Gunn's Avengers

Searching for his estranged sister who is homesteading in Dakota, Scottish clergyman Guthrie Gunn is bushwhacked and subsequently discovers that the same outlaws had previously killed all but one of his living relatives. Rescued by the Lakota, he finds his nephew living among them. Finding new faith after undergoing a Vision Quest, which shows him that his destiny is to seek out the villain, he embarks on a search for the wrongdoers, preaching his own quirky brand of religion along the way.

After seven years, he finds his way to Misery, Montana, where his enemies are now despotic lawmen. Gunn is joined by a motley band of avengers – including a Lakota tribesman, a reformed outlaw, a dime novelist, and two of the most notorious outlaws in the west – who will need all their diverse skills to stand a chance against the maniacal sheriff and his ruthless deputies.

Gunn's Avengers

Alvin Ford

A Black Horse Western

ROBERT HALE

© Alvin Ford 2019
First published in Great Britain 2019

ISBN 978-0-7198-2961-1

The Crowood Press
The Stable Block
Crowood Lane
Ramsbury
Marlborough
Wiltshire SN8 2HR

www.bhwesterns.com

Robert Hale is an imprint
of The Crowood Press

Typeset by
Derek Doyle & Associates, Shaw Heath
Printed and bound in Great Britain by
4Bind Ltd, Stevenage, SG1 2XT

PROLOGUE

My name is Frederick Abernathy and I fancy that I have had a little fame in my time, although it's not likely that you've heard of me.

I had pretensions to be a novelist, and I thought that I had some talent, but I lacked the most important requisite for success in that line – to wit, a wealthy wife. I had ambitions of being the next Fenimore Cooper, or the literary heir of Hawthorne, even the revered Herman Melville, but although a New York publisher was willing to pay me some twenty dollars for a novel that they added to their list, the reading public showed no inclination to buy it, let alone borrow it from a subscription library.

I thought that I was doomed to have to take up work as an articled clerk in some gloomy office somewhere, scrivening away my days recording other people's words. But then I discovered dime novels and they were the saving of me. They were easy to write, and although the pay for them was a pittance, it was considerably more income than I was then obtaining from any other source. You may be wondering, if you have read any of these dime novels, why you don't recognize my name as the author of any of them. Simply this: the publishers considered that Frederick Abernathy would be considered too much of a milksop to be able to write convincingly of derring-do and gunfighting, or about the hardships of pioneer settlers in rugged landscapes, so they changed my name to Flint Andrews, whom they considered sounded like a bull-chested fellow who would be at home roping steers or fighting Indians. Flint Andrews gained a popularity that Fred Abernathy had never obtained, but I was not satisfied. I was making a sufficient living, but I had to churn out work very quickly, to a preconceived formula, and I was eager for work that offered better rates of payment.

So when I received an invitation to go to Misery, Montana, to 'transcribe' the memoirs of its heroic sheriff, with an offer of an advance of $250 (a substantial sum of money in those days of the Rutherford B. Hayes Presidency), I jumped at the opportunity. To meet a man who seemed to be the greatest warrior in the west, the legend that was Nathan Bain, whose exploits had even been mentioned in the eastern press, with speculation that someday he would hold high office, perhaps even the highest office. How could I refuse? This man was paying me in one transaction more money than I had earned altogether in the previous five years. Little did I realize that it was the Devil's bargain.

But if I hadn't accepted the commission, I would never have met that mad Scottish preacher Guthrie Gunn, his nephew Brendan who had lived as a Sioux warrior, their companion Joseph, who was a Sioux warrior but recited Wordsworth and Coleridge, and I might never have learned the truth about Bain. Perhaps my own small contribution to this affair was decisive in the sheriff's undoing.

I will let other people judge that.

And I would never have met two of the most notorious outlaws in the west, who turned out to be splendid fellows, and far more honest than the man who called himself Nathan Bain.

I wrote about it years ago, back when the events were fresh in my mind, but the publishers took great liberties with my account, and rewrote Nathan Bain as the hero, and turned the true heroes of the matter into villains. If you should ever find *Mayhem in Montana* in a second-hand bookstore, be assured that this was not what I had originally written, and that mercenary publishers paid me my meagre fee for publication, and altered my words substantially.

The book you are now holding is the true story of what happened in Montana back in the autumn of 1878. Don't let anybody tell you any differently. I was there. I appear in this narrative, but I have chosen to write in the third person, because I was not present at much of the action, and writing it as a novel will allow me to portray events through the actions and thoughts of its principal actors. I heard their accounts of the events at the time, and those who are still among the living have corresponded with me recently to refresh my memory. My representation of the thoughts of the main villain of the story is speculative, but I interviewed him at length when I thought that I was assisting him with his memoirs, so I learned much of his character, and while my version of his thoughts and opinions is invented, I can assure you that it has the ring of truth. The actions of some other actors in the drama that I didn't observe personally can be confirmed or at least surmised from the testimony of the living witnesses.

This is the real story of what happened, how a motley band – a Scottish preacher named Guthrie Gunn, his nephew who lived as a Lakota warrior, a real Lakota buck who read English literature and played the piano, an emancipated slave turned outlaw (who then reformed), and yes, a humble dime novelist, and some others that we'll meet at their appropriate place in the story – faced up to the most corrupt sheriff in the west.

CHAPTER ONE

Kicking Buffalo's father had warned him many times about running off, but he never took any notice. He was always an early riser, and liked to make his way around the hunting grounds, learning the lie of the land. Just thirteen years old, he knew his destiny was to be a great warrior of the tribe.

As he scanned the landscape, he saw seven men approaching, walking, leading their horses slowly.

The five tepees of the hunting party were still, the braves all asleep. The men stopped short of the encampment. A tall man with a fat belly, and wearing an over-sized white hat, gave a signal. Kicking Buffalo ducked behind a grassy knoll, watching without being seen. A black man gathered the reins of all the horses, and held them. White Hat gave quiet orders to the other five men, who listened motionlessly. Kicking Buffalo was near enough to hear what the man was saying, but understood none of it.

The black man waited with the horses as the other men walked determinedly towards the five tepees in the encampment. With his gun hand, their white-hatted leader motioned, and the men entered the tepees.

The boy watched with horror. The white-hatted man went into the central tepee, the bigger one, where Kicking Buffalo knew his father was sleeping. Another man followed White Hat into the tepee, and then there were four shots. Simultaneously, a fusillade of many shots echoed throughout the encampment, the explosions barely muffled by the tepees' buffalo-hide coverings. The boy desperately hoped that his father hadn't been killed. Mighty Bull could easily dispatch the white men, given half a chance.

But the men came out of the tepee, not looking backwards, so the boy knew that Mighty Bull must have been killed.

Kicking Buffalo knew that he should keep quiet, and let the men ride away, but he couldn't help himself. He cried out, and ran forward. The men turned to look at him, then gave uneasy glances at each other. Two of them rushed him and grabbed him roughly by the arms. Struggle as he might, they held him fast.

The black man approached White Hat and spoke to him. Kicking Buffalo could hear that the black man was talking agitatedly. He saw the big man looking at him, a cold scowl on his face. There was a barked command to the underling, who shook his head. White Hat shouted, his face full of fury. The black man shook his head again. White Hat unholstered his gun and pressed it against the man's forehead. Shrugging dejectedly, the black man hurried off towards his horse, collected some items from his saddle-bag, then turned and strode towards the boy.

Desperately, Kicking Buffalo leaned over and bit one of his captors on the arm. The man screamed and let go of him. With his right hand now free, he punched the other man holding him square on the nose. The man released the boy, and his hands went up to his face. Kicking Buffalo ran, fast as he could. He didn't dare look backwards, because that would slow him down, maybe making the difference between escape or death.

The black man was too fast for him, however. Knowing that the man was almost upon him, he wheeled around, took the prized knife that his father had given him, and slashed out towards the man. He managed to cut him on the arm, but then something went over his head, blinding him, and he felt a shuddering pain as something hit him hard on the jaw.

Then he felt nothing.

The Brennans' wagon drove along the trail, skirting the edge of the reservation. Often, William Brennan made the trip alone, but this time Martha went to market too, leaving Brendan and Beth in the charge of Sissy, the daughter of their neighbours, the Duggans.

Although the trail passed close to the reservation, William rarely encountered any Sioux on these trips, but when he did they always showed friendliness towards him, and he'd even picked up a few words of Lakota. He'd never seen any trouble.

Martha put her hand above her eyes to shade them from the sun, and said, 'Is that smoke in the distance?'

'Looks like it. We'll see what it is when we clear this ridge.'

A few minutes later, they could see that there was an encampment of tepees in the distance, all of them on fire.

'Sweet mother of God,' William said. 'What's happened here?'

'William, we must stop to help,' his wife said.

William brought the wagon to a halt at the trail's closest point to the burning encampment.

'Stay here, Martha,' he said, as he stepped down from the wagon, then ran towards the tepees. The stench was overpowering. The central tepee had burnt to the ground, and there were charred remains of tribesmen lying inside the outline of the ruin.

He walked to the other tepees, which had not yet completely burnt down. It was obviously a party of braves from the Sioux reservation. Some of these bodies were not burnt, but they had been shot at point-blank range. Everyone was dead, William was certain of that. He thought it was unlikely that an enemy tribe would have committed a massacre as brutal as this. It had to be the work of white men.

There were no horses nearby, but William saw many hoofmarks. The horse tracks led to the trail, then headed west along it. All this killing just to steal some horses? William shook his head in disgust.

There was nothing that he could do to put out the fires, so he walked back to the wagon. He saw that his wife had jumped down, and was looking around.

'What is it, Martha?'

'I heard something.'

Brennan listened, only hearing the crackling of the fire. 'Maybe you imagined it.'

'I definitely heard moaning.'

William listened, and then nodded. A ditch ran alongside the trail for a few hundred yards. He jumped nimbly down to the lower ground, and looked along it.

He shouted up to Martha. 'There's some kind of

bundle along a bit. Seems to be moving. I'm going to look at it. You stay here.'

He set off along the ditch, and came to a large sack, tied at the top, with some kind of bundle in it. The bundle groaned, and moved slightly. He took the knotted cord that was holding the end of the sack closed and untied it. Opening the sack, Brennan found that the bundle was a boy.

'Sweet Jesus!' Martha said from directly above, not having obeyed her husband's instruction.

He said, 'It's a boy, looks like he's one of the party here. Somebody has put him in a sack and thrown him in the ditch. Left him for dead.'

'But he's not dead?'

'If he is, he's the noisiest corpse I ever heard.'

Brennan slipped the sack off the boy, pulling him free of it.

'Is he conscious?' Martha asked.

'I don't think so.' Brennan took the boy's shoulders in his hands, and lifted him gently. 'There's some blood on his clothing.'

William shook the boy gently. His eyes opened, then widened in alarm. He started pounding his fists against Brennan's chest. Brennan took the boy's wrists in his hands, holding them firmly.

'Who did this to you, boy?'

The boy struggled to get free of Brennan's tight grip.

'I'm not going to hurt you. Who did this?'

Martha jumped down into the ditch, and showed herself to the boy. Her husband let go of the lad's arms, and let Martha approach him. He seemed to be taken aback to see a woman.

13

'I can't imagine what you must have gone through,' she said, stroking the boy's cheek.

The boy began to speak, quickly and agitatedly, in the Lakota language. Martha knew no words of Lakota at all, and William only a few. She looked up at him, but he shook his head.

Martha spoke soothingly to the boy, knowing that the words didn't matter, but that her tone would convey that she was not his enemy.

The boy spoke more slowly. The only word that Brennan could understand was '*wasicun*', the Lakota word for a white man. The boy used the word several times, getting more agitated as he repeated it.

Martha examined him for injuries and saw that there was a knife wound on his leg, not deep, but needing treatment.

'Poor child,' she said. 'What are we going to do with him?'

'I don't know. It's a fair way to the main reservation encampment from here. If we turned up with a wounded child, we could find ourselves getting rough treatment from his tribesmen. They're peaceable, if they think we mean no harm. But if we take him there, we could be in trouble.'

'What can we do then? Has nobody else in the camp survived?'

William shook his head.

'We can't just leave him,' she said. 'He could die out here. Maybe we should take him home with us.'

William agreed, and Martha climbed back out of the ditch. Then he lifted the boy up in his arms, lifted him out, and stepped up himself. Then they put him in the back of the wagon, Martha sitting with him, and they continued on their way homeward.

The boy recovered well at the Brennan farm.

His wound was not as bad as Martha had feared. There was no doctor nearby, but Martha had a book about basic medical treatments and she washed his wound and stitched it up carefully.

Right from the start, she treated him as if he were one of the family. When he was well enough to sit up, Beth, her four-year-old daughter, would climb on his lap and sing to him in her piping voice. And Brendan, who at the age of twelve was perhaps one or two years younger than the lad, set about the task of teaching him English.

When the boy knew enough English to be able to converse with them, Martha asked him his name. He told her, but it was full of odd consonants and strange vowels, and she just couldn't reproduce it, as hard as she tried.

She said, 'I wish I could say your name, but I can't. Would you mind if I gave you a name?'

The boy smiled. 'In my tribe, we get different names as we get older. When I was a small boy, I was . . .' – and he said something incomprehensible – 'and when I grew older they called me . . .' – yet again, the name he had told them before. 'Now that I have a new life here with you, I should have a different name.'

Martha smiled. 'I shall call you Joseph.'

'Joseph?' the boy said. 'Joseph.' He repeated the name slowly, as if trying it out for size.

'Joseph, Joseph,' Beth said. 'A good new name for my new brother. You are my brother, aren't you, Joseph?'

Joseph smiled. 'Yes, if you'll have me. I never had a

sister back on the reserve—' stumbling over the long word.

Brendan completed it for him. 'Reservation.'

'*Reversation*,' Beth said.

'Reservation,' Joseph said. 'Or a brother either. But now that I live here with you, I have both.'

Martha hadn't thought that they would be adopting the boy they had rescued from the massacre, but that was what appeared to be happening.

'Is Joseph a good name?' the newly named Joseph asked. 'What does it mean?'

'Mean?' said Brendan. 'It doesn't mean anything. It's just your name.'

Joseph looked puzzled. 'In my tribe, our names always meant something.'

'What did your old name mean, then?' asked Beth.

Joseph thought for a moment. 'I don't know. You haven't taught me the English words for it yet.'

'Then it doesn't mean anything, silly,' Beth said. 'Just like Joseph.'

Martha said, 'That's not quite right, Beth. Joseph does mean something.'

'Really, mommy?' the girl said. 'What does it mean?'

'It means "God increases".'

Joseph was puzzled by this. He didn't know if this was a good name or not. What was 'God'?

'Do your names mean anything?' he asked.

Martha said, 'My name means "lady". Beth is short for "Elizabeth", which means "the fullness of God".'

That word 'God' again.

'What does Brenbren mean?' Beth asked.

Martha laughed. 'It means that you couldn't pronounce

"Brendan" when you were learning to talk. His full name is Brendan Michael Brennan, but all you could manage to say was "Brenbren". I thought it was so cute that I kept using it, until he told me to stop. Brendan means prince.'

'That's silly,' Beth said. 'Brenbren's not a prince.'

'How do you know?' Brendan asked. 'Pa's always saying he's descended from the High Kings of Ireland. That would make me a prince.'

'Then I must be a princess,' Beth said.

William came in then from working in the barn, and wasn't quite sure what they were talking about.

He said, 'Princess or not, I can tan your hide if you don't behave.'

But Beth knew he was joking.

Quite by accident, the boy who had been Kicking Buffalo became Joseph Brennan.

There was no school nearby, so Martha educated her children herself, and included Joseph in all the lessons. She taught him to read, initially along with Beth, but he was so quick to learn that soon he was more proficient than Brendan. Martha let him read freely from her library, and he devoured the books. She was not surprised that he liked Fenimore Cooper. She thought he would realize that the Delaware tribesmen depicted in *The Last of the Mohicans* were natives like himself, although she thought it unlikely that he would know the tribe. She was also not surprised when he told her that he thought Mr Longfellow's poem *The Song of Hiawatha* was ridiculous.

Martha felt guilty about not trying to return the boy to his people. Now that Joseph spoke English with total fluency, he could tell his tribesmen that the Brennans had helped him. She asked whether he wanted to return to his tribe, and he said that he didn't. This was surprising, but she was glad that he was now part of their family.

On their visits to town to buy supplies, they never learned anything about the massacre. Nobody seemed to talk about it, as if it had never happened.

As the years went by, Brendan and Joseph lost their boyishness, and grew up strong and muscular. When they didn't have lessons, they helped on the farm. Brendan frequently expressed the opinion that when he grew up he wanted to be a Lakota brave, just like his brother, to which William and Martha just laughed. Joseph never spoke of his ambitions for manhood. He never told them that his dreams were haunted by White Hat. Although he loved learning and reading for its own sake, he had an ulterior motive. Knowledge would help him to track down that man and his gang, and have revenge on them.

In the late afternoon on an unseasonably warm April day in 1870, Martha and Beth were indoors, where the shade made the air a little cooler. William had just come back to the house after tending the fields for most of the afternoon.

Brendan and Joseph didn't waste the time before dinner by sitting indoors like women. Joseph had been teaching Brendan the use of bow and arrow. He had been learning it himself before his life had so abruptly changed, and – partly from memory, and partly from a book about woodcraft – he had made a bow, and a plentiful supply of arrows. He often practised, using a target William had built him, just like one he had seen illustrated in a book about Robin Hood. He loved the story of the archery contest in Nottingham, especially when Robin Hood won by splitting another arrow down the middle. Mr Hood must have had Lakota blood in him.

Brendan had watched Joseph's archery practice, and had wanted to learn to do it. So Joseph made another bow for him, and taught him to use it. He had only been practising for a few weeks, but he was now hitting on or near the centre of the target more often than not.

Their archery arena was in a hollow two hundred yards from the farmhouse, where they could practise for hours without anybody seeing them. Joseph knew that Brendan didn't want any 'palefaces', as he called his parents and sister, watching them.

They were just about to stop, when they heard some men riding up.

'That's strange,' Brendan said. 'We never get any visitors.'

Joseph and Brendan went to the edge of the hollow, and raised their heads up to ground level to see what was happening.

Five riders approached the farmhouse. They stopped a little short of it, and dismounted. One gathered the reins of the horses, holding them. The four others began to walk towards the farmhouse, slowly and deliberately, looking around as they did so. Joseph and Brendan ducked down again so as not to be seen.

Joseph had a very bad feeling.

'What's happening?' Brendan said.

'Shh,' Joseph said. 'We could be in big trouble if we make any noise.'

'Who are these guys?' Brendan whispered.

'I don't know,' Joseph said. But he did know.

One of the men knocked at the door. William opened it, saw the men, and spoke. The man drew his gun, pressed it into William's chest, and squeezed the trigger. William fell back with the impact. Another shot went into him as he lay on the ground.

Then the men rushed into the house.

Brendan tried to climb out of the hollow. But Joseph pulled him back.

'Stay down. We don't stand a chance. We only have bows and arrows, and these guys have guns.'

'But we can't let them do this. What about Ma and Beth?'

Four more shots sounded from inside the house in quick succession.

'We can't do anything,' Joseph said. 'If we try it, we'll only end up dead.'

'But Pa . . . and Ma . . . and Beth.' Brendan choked back sobs.

'There's nothing we can do. All we can do is stay alive, find out who these men are and why they've done this, and get revenge on them.'

'We can fight them now,' Brendan said.

'No. We'd only end up dead.'

The men came back out of the house. The boys had their heads just enough above ground level at the top of the hollow to be able to see the men, without themselves being seen.

Joseph was already sure who these men were, but a clear view of their faces confirmed it. Two of them, he couldn't forget. They were a tall, heavy-set man with a white hat, and a black man. They had massacred his real father and the rest of them at the encampment. The black man had thrust him into a sack and left him for dead.

He almost cried out. He wanted to leap from the hollow and put arrows through both of these men's hearts. But he stopped himself. He would likely miss, and even if he didn't, he couldn't kill all five of the men here, and most likely he and Brendan would end up dead.

To stop himself from screaming, he forced his knuckles into his mouth, and with his other hand he pulled Brendan down, sat on top of him, and covered his mouth, so that he wouldn't call out.

After a time, he heard the men riding away.

When the sound quietened, Joseph let go of Brendan, and they both got up and ran to the house. William was dead, sure enough, shot once in the heart and once in the head. Joseph ran past William's corpse, and in the parlour Martha and Beth were also bullet-riddled and lifeless.

Brendan caught up with him, dashed to his mother's body, and shook it, as if that would revive her. Tears streamed down his face.

Joseph just stood there and watched, grief welling up in him too. Brendan looked up at Joseph as if he were ashamed of his tears. Joseph said nothing.

'What do we do now?' Brendan asked.

Joseph pondered a moment. 'We can't report this to the authorities. They'll take one look at me and think that I had something to do with it.'

'Not if I tell them otherwise.'

'According to most *wasicun*, I'm a filthy redskin. They'd pin it on me for sure. You're just a kid. So am I, but I'm a stinking savage as far as they're concerned. No. We'll hunt these men down, and we'll get revenge on them for what they've done to us. But we can't do it yet. We need to be older.'

'What do we do, then?'

'First of all, we'll bury Ma and Pa and Beth. Then we'll take what supplies we can and we'll go to the reservation.'

Although the outlaws hadn't stolen anything from the house and left the family's elderly horses, robbery may well have been their motive; they just probably hadn't realized the Brennans didn't have anything worth stealing. Not yet, but someday, somebody was going to pay.

They buried their parents and sister, took what provisions they could from the larder, and all the guns and ammunition from their father's armoury, and prepared to set out for Kicking Buffalo's home.

Joseph had no trouble finding the reservation. When the Brennans had taken him in, he had no idea where their farm was, but he had studied the atlas that Martha had in her library and he knew now exactly where the reservation was located. William Brennan's compass made it even easier to find. Two days' ride took them there.

The tribe were astonished to see the boy that they thought had died in the massacre. The brutal deaths of so many tribesmen had been a mystery to them, and now that they had an account from Kicking Buffalo about what had happened, they had some understanding at last of the circumstances.

As Joseph had told him before they set off, the tribesmen accepted Brendan as one of their own, because he was Kicking Buffalo's brother. They renamed Kicking Buffalo now, as Red Ghost, and Brendan naturally became

Pale Ghost.

As Brendan lived with the tribe, and came to manhood, he realized bitterly that he had attained his wish to grow up to be a Lakota warrior.

CHAPTER TWO

Gunn rode easily along the trail in southern Dakota, now finally getting comfortable with the western saddle, somewhat different from those he had used in Scotland, now even accustomed to the pommel, which the livery man had told him was often used to hold a rope for lassoing cattle. He was in his late forties, with thick greying hair, with bushy eyebrows that still showed a touch of the fiery red hair of his youth. When he could, he would make sure that he shaved his whiskers every day – if he didn't he would find a salt-and-pepper mixture of red and white hair in his moustache and beard. He had a firm mouth and hooded eyes, which made him seem wary and suspicious of strangers, but he had an easy manner, learned over several years of sermonizing to his congregation from the pulpit.

The Reverend Doctor Guthrie Gunn D.D. (Doctor of Divinity), formerly the Kirk minister in the parish of Tollcross, a village near Glasgow in Scotland, was now travelling far from home in hopes of a reunion with his estranged sister, Martha.

He knew from her occasional letters that she and her

husband had left Boston some years ago to become farmers in Dakota. The family had been sundered apart by her marriage to an Irishman, and worse, a Catholic. Gunn had not spoken to her since the day she had announced her intention to marry William Brennan and convert to his faith. Guthrie and Martha had been close as children, but her conversion to the Popish religion had been too much for him. He had thought that he would never make contact with her again, and although their mother had replied to her letters, he had not.

But circumstances change. Gunn had lost his wife to child-bed fever, and their sickly infant son had only lived for three days after his birth. Inconsolable with grief, Gunn had been unable to continue as the parish minister, and had turned against a God who could rob him of his family.

Drink had dulled the pain. He spent months in a daze, rarely if ever sober. Soon, he found himself evicted from the manse by the Kirk Session, and he drifted for months in a daze.

On the occasions when he *was* sober, he stayed with his widowed mother in Shawlands in the south of Glasgow, in the two-storey terraced house that had been bought for her after her husband's death by her father, a bluff Yorkshire merchant who had accepted his daughter's conversion from Anglicanism to the Presbyterian faith when she had met the handsome and young clergyman Andrew Gunn, who was on a walking holiday in the Yorkshire dales. His mother was unhappy that Guthrie had lost his faith, but supported him as best she could. Unfortunately, she was elderly and in failing health, and she succumbed to pneumonia in the winter of 1868.

His mother's estate, which was sizable, was left to her two children. This circumstance sobered up Gunn considerably, although he was not yet ready to accept the existence of a God who could kill his wife and child before their time.

He decided that he would travel in search of his sister to inform her of their mother's death and the inheritance to which she was entitled. Since he no longer believed in the teachings of the Church of Scotland, he had lost much of the bitterness against the Roman Church and its followers. If Presbyterians were mistaken, then the Catholics were no worse for also being wrong. Time, he decided, to attempt a reconciliation. There had been no letters from Martha in the last four years, so Gunn decided to make the transatlantic crossing to visit her in person.

Once his finances were organized, he took passage by steamship from Greenock to Boston, Massachusetts. The railways – railroads, as the Americans called them – were beginning to make inroads into the heartland of the continent, and he took the train as far as it would take him, then onward by stagecoach, and then he was able to buy a horse and some supplies. When he bought the horse he asked about the whereabouts of the Brennan farm, which he'd heard was some way west of the town. Bill Higgs, the livery man, was intrigued by the traveller, because of his strange accent, which he thought was Irish, and because of his clerical collar.

'I'm looking for kin,' Gunn said. 'Mrs Brennan is my sister.'

'You don't say,' Higgs said.

'I do say, because she is.'

'I heard tell that the Brennans were dead.'

'No!' Gunn exclaimed. Not another bereavement, on top of all the others. 'What happened?'

'It's a mystery. Folks from a neighbouring farm rode to visit with them, but just found three shallow graves, marked with three simple crosses.'

'Dear God!' Gunn said.

'There was no grave for the Brennan boy, though. Whoever did it may have kidnapped him. There was rumours that they had a redskin boy staying with them. Some folks reckon the savage kid killed them, high-tailed it back to the reservation, stole some horses. But it were only rumours. . . .'

'Did nobody investigate?' Gunn asked.

'Can't say that they did. Things like that happen hereabouts.'

'Well, I want to go there and see for myself. Will you sell me a horse?'

'I'll let you have a good horse for fifteen dollars.'

After giving it some consideration, Gunn shook on it, and said, 'It's a deal.'

'That includes saddle and pack. It'll maybe take two days to get where you're going. And you should be careful. The trail borders on the Sioux reservation. They don't often go to the edge of the reservation, but you never know.'

'They won't trouble a peaceable man of God.'

'You can't trust these savages.'

Gunn said, 'I'll keep my eyes open, and my gun loaded. Once I buy a gun, that is.'

Gunn made swift progress across the landscape, making good time on the second day, thinking that he would reach the neighbourhood of the Brennan farm at about dusk.

'Well, lookee here,' said a voice.

He must have dozed off slightly in the saddle, because he had not seen the horsemen approaching. But there were five of them right in front of him.

'Good afternoon, gentlemen,' Gunn said. 'Am I on the right road for the Brennan farm?'

The man who had spoken previously, a stocky man with a white Stetson, spoke again. 'Yah talk funny, mister. And yuh've got one of those back to front collars that preachers wear. Are yuh some kind of priest?'

'Not I, sir. I'm a minister of the Church of Scotland.'

'In my book that makes yuh a priest.'

'Not exactly. We don't approve of priests and their Popish ways. . . .'

'Yuh don't *approve*?' The man snorted, finding Gunn amusing. '*Yuh don't approve*. Well, maybe I *don't approve* of you. What do yuh say to that, mister priest?'

Gunn said, 'I'd be obliged if you would let me be about my business.'

The white-hatted man glanced at the black man on the horse beside him, and smiled. Then he turned to give Gunn a hard, mean stare.

'If yuh're looking for the Brennan farm, then it is my business.'

'Why's that?'

'Because the Brennan farm is gone. They sold up their farm, sold it to the Diamond Deuce Ranch. They left this territory years ago.'

'I heard they were dead and buried.'

'What I heard, they didn't like living so near to the

28

reservation, and decided to move further west.'

'And who might you be, that you know so much about it?'

'That wouldn't be any of your business. But I work for the Diamond Deuce, and pretty soon you'll be trespassing.'

'I'd really like to speak to somebody who knows something about the Brennans.'

'And why would you want to do that?'

'Mrs Brennan is my sister, her family are the only kin I have left.'

'Is that so?' The man eased his horse nearer to the black man beside him and whispered in his ear.

Then he turned to Gunn again. 'We've got to be about our business just now, but my . . . associate will take yuh where you need to go.'

'That's obliging of you,' Gunn said.

'*Obliging*? Humph.' The large man rode on, and three of the other riders followed. The black man stayed, and waited until the other riders had gone some distance. Then he turned and beckoned for Gunn to follow.

Gunn rode up and positioned his horse alongside the other rider, and they set off slowly.

'It's very good of you to go to this trouble for me, sir.'

The man laughed.

'What's so funny?'

'I'm not used to being called "sir". "Boy", I get that a lot. . . .'

'I take it that you used to be a slave.'

'I did. Then Abraham Lincoln passed a law that emancipated me, and his Union Army won a war against the people that didn't want to emancipate me. So then they had to.'

'I'm pleased that that you're a free man,' Gunn said.

'Oh, I'm not free. But I'm not a slave either. I still have to do what I'm told – but now I have to like it.'

'I feel sorry for you.'

'Don't feel sorry for me. Feel sorry for yourself.' The man paused, and climbed down from the saddle. 'We have to dismount here.'

Gunn was puzzled. 'Why should I feel sorry for myself? And why do we have to dismount?'

The man took the reins of the clergyman's mount. 'Just dismount, sir, and I'll explain.'

Gunn swung his leg over the horse, then dropped to the ground.

'What do you have to explain?'

'This.' The black man slipped his gun swiftly from its holster, moved its barrel into his other hand, and with one sure movement brought the gun butt down on the Scotsman's head, very hard.

Then Gunn was no longer aware of anything.

CHAPTER THREE

Red Ghost and Pale Ghost were riding at the very border of the reservation, near the spot where Red Ghost had survived the massacre.

Pale Ghost never understood why his brother visited this place so often. He knew that even if it were possible to visit the site of the Brennan farm, he would not want to do it. It would remind him too much of what he had lost.

Red Ghost came often, to keep the hatred alive. To remind himself. Pale Ghost had only lost one family, whereas Red Ghost had lost two.

'I need to look,' he told Pale Ghost. 'I need to remember their faces, so I'll know them again when I find them.'

'I only saw them once. There were two or three of them that I didn't see clearly, but the two who seemed to be the leaders – I would know them anywhere.'

'I saw them twice. I would know those two in an instant.'

'Have you had enough for today, Red?'

'Yes. Let's go back.'

But as he was about to turn his mount around, Red Ghost had a strange sensation, that someone was near. He scanned the landscape, but couldn't see anything.

'What are you looking for?'

'Shh.'

'But. . . .'

'Quiet. I *felt* something, but I couldn't see anything. But now I think that I hear it.'

'I don't hear anything.'

'You're a Lakota by chance and by training. Not by birth.'

'Well if you're going to . . .'

'Quiet!'

Pale Ghost got the message, and shut up.

'It's a man, groaning.'

'I don't hear anything,' Pale Ghost said. 'Wait a minute. Now I hear it. Where is it coming from?'

Red Ghost cupped his ear with his hand. Then pointed. 'It's coming from the ditch. The exact spot where your parents – our parents – found me after the massacre.'

'Let's go and look.'

The two dismounted and ran to the ditch. Red Ghost laid one hand down on the edge and eased himself down to the lower level, Pale Ghost following a moment later.

Red looked along the trench, saw something moving, and ran the few short steps towards it. It was a sack, very like the one that he had been found in by the Brennans. He knew it was the same size because he had the one that he had been found in. When he discovered that the Brennans had kept it, he had insisted on having it. He had it still, rigged up in his tepee, so that he could look at it every day.

Two legs dangled out of the opening of the sack. Kicking Buffalo, as he had been known then, had been fully inside the sack, but this victim was much larger. Red loosened the sack, pulled it free from its victim, and had a look at him. He was a middle-aged man, with grey hair and full whiskers. There was a book resting on his chest. Red picked it up and looked at it.

'A Bible. Just like one Ma used to have.'

'He's wearing a dog collar,' Pale Ghost said.

'What? For putting a leash on?'

'No. It's just called that. It means he's some kind of clergyman. You know, like the priest Ma took you to when you got baptised.'

Red Ghost frowned, thinking of when the Brennan family had been intact. 'I remember. But that man had some funny clothes.'

'Vestments and a chasuble. That's what catholic priests wear.'

'This man's got a suit, and some kind of black tunic, and this kind of hoop around his neck.'

Pale Ghost nodded. 'That hoop is the dog collar. It's how we know he's a Christian minister. Can't tell what denomination, though. Might be a Presbyterian, like Ma used to be before she met Pa and converted.'

'I never really understood that,' Red Ghost said. 'How can people of the same religion be so different in their beliefs.'

'Ma talked to me about it when I asked her about her life in Scotland, before she met Pa. Her father was a minister of the Presbyterian church, and so was her brother. They don't believe that the bread and wine in the Holy Communion turns into the body and blood of Christ.'

'I never really believed that either.'

'You never said.'

'It would have upset Ma. I wasn't sure about Christ

33

coming back from the dead either.'

'You *are* a heathen savage.'

'I hope you're joking, *wasicun*. Apart from your ghastly pallor, you look every inch the Lakota warrior.'

'Ghastly pallor,' Pale Ghost shook his head. 'You've read too many books.'

'Nothing wrong with books.'

The clergyman groaned, and mumbled in his unconscious state. Red Ghost thought that his black tunic was looking stained, and loosened it to take a look.

'He's bleeding.'

'Is it bad?'

'I can't tell. There's a gash just below his heart, but I can't tell how deep it is.'

'What shall we do with him?' asked Pale Ghost.

'Take him to the reservation,' Red Ghost said. 'Look after him. Like the story in the Bible about the Samaritan. Let's lift him out of the ditch. You could wait with him while I go to the reservation and get some of the men to come and help. I'd only be gone a couple of hours.'

'What if the men who did this come back?'

'You're Pale Ghost. You can fight them. But I doubt they'll come back.'

'Do you reckon it's the same men?'

'I think they must be. This man has been treated exactly the same way that I was.'

They lifted the man out of the ditch, and brought him away from the trail, just over the brow of a low mound, so that they couldn't be seen if anybody should happen to pass that way.

Then without another word, Red mounted his horse, and rode off towards the reservation.

Gunn woke up, and wished that he hadn't. He had a searing headache. He opened his eyes, then closed them again, trying to shut out the pain. The wound below his chest hurt, too.

He opened his eyes again, and looked around. A young man was standing over him. He was dressed in the garb of a Lakota buck, all beads and buckskin. His hair was long in the fashion of the native tribesmen, but his was fair and not dark. And he was white.

'Where am I, laddie?' he said, a little more clearly.

'You're in the Lakota reservation. We found you with a sack over your head, in a ditch.'

'We?'

'My brother and me.'

'What's your name, boy?'

'Pale Ghost.'

Gunn laughed, but it hurt, and he started to choke. When he had recovered, he said, 'You're certainly pale. I take it you were captured by the Indians.'

'No sir. My family were killed by outlaws. We think you were set upon by the very same men.'

'We?'

'My brother and me.'

'Is he white like you?'

'No sir. He's Lakota. He was left for dead some years back in the very same ditch we found you. He was put in a sack, just like you were. . . .'

'Sack. What sack?'

'We found you in a burlap sack, and you were bleeding. Red Ghost rode to get the tribesmen to come and help you.'

35

'Red Ghost? That your brother?'

'Yes sir. We're not blood kin, but my parents found him in that same ditch, and took him in and adopted him unofficially. We escaped when Ma and Pa and my sister were killed by the same men. I came to the reservation with him, and I've become a Lakota warrior.'

'How old are you, boy?'

'I'm not sure. The Lakota don't measure the days with our calendar, so I haven't got an accurate measure. What's the date, sir?'

'If this is the same day that I was bushwhacked. . . .'

'It is.'

'Then it's March the fourth. The year's 1873.'

'Then I'm eighteen. I was born on February the second, 1855.'

Gunn stared at the boy. 'What's your name? I don't mean Pale Ghost. What's your Christian name?'

'My name was Brendan Michael Brennan.'

'*Holy God*!' Gunn exclaimed.

'What is it, sir?'

Gunn tried to sit up, but the pain was still too much for him to move very much. He lay back again, and said, 'My name is Guthrie Gunn. My sister was Martha Elizabeth Gunn. She married an Irishman named William Brennan.'

Pale Ghost gasped.

Gunn was shaking, or shivering. He croaked out, 'I'm your uncle.'

'I don't believe it,' Pale Ghost said.

'It's one hell of a cosmic joke. If there is a God, he must really have it in for us.'

'You're my Uncle Guthrie?'

36

'Yes.'

There was a sudden shaft of light, as the tepee entrance flapped open. Gunn was now sufficiently aware of his surroundings to realize where he was. A shadow fell over him a moment later.

He looked up and saw a young man around the same age and build as his nephew, dressed much the same, but this boy had the colouring of a Lakota tribesman.

'Red, this man is my uncle.'

Gunn saw the boy look at him in astonishment, then turn again quizzically to Pale Ghost.

'He's Guthrie Gunn. Ma's brother.'

'Pleased to meet you, sir,' said the Lakota boy. 'The uncle of my brother is my uncle, too.'

'Your brother said you were adopted by my sister. Did she give you a Christian name?'

'Yes sir. I was baptised in the Catholic church as Joseph Brennan.'

'*The Catholic church?*' Gunn spluttered. 'She *would* do that. Oh well, I suppose that's as good a baptism as any. Joseph Brennan, you say? Joseph?'

'Yes sir.'

'I don't like it. Sounds too Irish.'

'It *is* Irish.'

'Well, it'll have to do. Do you mind if I call you Joseph?'

'No sir. Lakota people have many different names. I've had more names than some. I'm now known as Red Ghost, because I came back from the dead. Brendan is Pale Ghost, because he turned up along with me. And he's pale. . . .'

'I get it, laddie.'

'I used to be known as Kicking Buffalo. . . .'

'Was that because they thought you kicked like a buffalo?'

'No, sir. I tried to kick a buffalo. Then I was Joseph Brennan, and now Red Ghost.'

Gunn shook his head again, but stopped when he realized it was hurting. 'And you're baptised as a Catholic?'

'I'm not really a Christian, sir.'

Gunn said, 'I don't suppose that I am, strictly speaking, anymore.'

'I'll answer to Joseph for you, my uncle.'

'I'm not your uncle. Ah, what the hell, what does it matter? If you're not a Christian, after having been baptised, especially by the Papists, I like ye all the better for it. My name's Guthrie.'

'Very well, Mr Guthrie.'

Gunn laughed, 'Just Guthrie, laddie.'

Joseph frowned. 'But I thought that all male elders were addressed so.'

'Where'd ye learn that?'

'I read it in a book, sir . . . Guthrie.'

'You read books then, Joseph?'

'Yes, sir. I read all of your sister's books, after she taught me to read.'

'Even the Bible?'

'Yes. King James and the Douay.'

'The Douay is a bit doubtful. It's translated from the Vulgate.'

'Sir?'

'Never mind. What did you make of the King James?'

'Very exciting. I was a bit puzzled by the numbered paragraphs. . . .'

'They're called verses, laddie.'

Joseph pondered. 'But they're nothing like the verses in the Keats and Wordsworth books that I read.'

Gunn wondered what kind of world he had woken up into, where an Indian buck was discussing English poetry with him.

The boy continued: 'Then I read Milton's *Paradise Lost*, and every tenth line in that book was numbered, and I realized that it was so you could keep a note of your place. So you could tell somebody which bit of the Bible to read, and they could find it from the numbers.' Joseph smiled. 'I liked that book, the story was a bit like the beginning of the Bible. Do you think Mr Milton had read it, sir?'

Gunn spluttered, then laughed out loud. 'I'm sure of it.'

Joseph nodded. 'I thought so.'

'Tell me something, laddie?'

'What's that, sir?'

'Is there somewhere around here that I can get something to eat? I'm starving.'

Gunn stayed with the Lakota for about eighteen months. He was weak to begin with, but the medicine man gave him some potions, spoke some strange chants over him, and he recovered. He didn't know if these remedies were more effective than the quackery that passed for medicine in Scotland, but he thought they might be. After a few weeks, he was up and riding with his nephews (it seemed only right to accept Joseph as being as much his nephew as Brendan), and learning the ways of the Lakota.

They were civilized people. Not in the strange way that Joseph was civilized, with his odd book-learning, but in their own way, and had been so for hundreds, perhaps thousands of years. Back when his ancestors had been brutish illiterate Picts, these tribal people had been living peaceably, in harmony with nature. They had a generosity of spirit towards him, which was more than most Scotsmen had ever shown him.

They lived in a large encampment, spread over several acres, with many tepees, too numerous for Gunn to be able to count and get the same figure each time. The encampment was set in a barren plain, with looming hills in the distance. Once he was recovered from the ordeal inflicted on him by the bushwhackers, he walked around the encampment. The people were friendly towards him, although he was unable to communicate with them without the help of Brendan or Joseph.

He liked the company of his nephew and his 'brother', and he spoke often with the tribal chief, with translations by Brendan or Joseph, and discussed religion in the same manner with the medicine man. Gunn had tried to make some headway with the Lakota language, but he was too old or too stupid to learn it. Brendan was fluent, though.

Gunn knew that he would never fit in here, although he had doubts about fitting in anywhere else. The chief, who went by the splendid name that translated into English as Charging Bull, made it plain that he was welcome to stay. The medicine man was also an agreeable chap, as much clergyman as purveyor of healing, perhaps more so.

Raises Horses, the medicine man, understood that Gunn was a clergyman in one of the Christian denominations, and although he'd scorned missionaries who had come to convert the red-skinned heathens, he liked Gunn. Gunn had doubts, and that was good.

Gunn had seen Raises Horses take young men out to

the hills, and the youngsters came back transfigured, much like the Bible story about Christ looking different when coming back to his disciples (Matthew Chapter 17 Verse 2 – Gunn knew from memory). Gunn had asked about this, and Raises Horses told him that it was the Vision Quest. Gunn had never heard of this, and the medicine man explained that it was a method of seeking guidance from the spirit world. Gunn was sceptical of this, thinking that it must be some kind of superstitious mumbo-jumbo, but when Brendan and Joseph told him they had undergone the ritual, he changed his mind.

Gunn asked if he could undergo the ritual, too. He had come to the conclusion that if this alien ritual could give him some new insight into the state of his soul, it would be worth attempting.

Raises Horses understood that Gunn was also a medicine man of his tribe, and after some consideration, and discussion with Charging Bull, concluded that it would do the Scotsman good.

It was a serious matter to allow a *wasicun* to undertake the ritual. Charging Bull and the shaman questioned Gunn thoroughly. It was clear that Gunn was unlike the previous men with hoops around their necks. He was not dogmatic about his own God, and was interested in the truth.

So the shaman and the chief agreed that Gunn would undertake the Vision Quest.

CHAPTER FOUR

Raises Horses had prepared Gunn, led him through the ritual, with the preparatory cleansing in the sweat box, and (with Joseph translating) explained what had to be done in the ritual itself. The procedure of the ritual is sacred, and must not be revealed to any *wasicun*, so when Frederick Abernathy discussed it with Gunn some years later, the clergyman would reveal nothing of the details.

'I've got too much respect for the Lakota and their ways, Fred,' he had said, 'to tell you of the details of the ritual. I made them a solemn vow that I would never talk about it to a white man. I shouldn't even really tell you what I saw, but what happened afterwards don't make sense without knowing what was in the vision.'

During the ritual, which lasted for two days, Gunn experienced a vision, which may have been a dream, although he was convinced he was awake during it. He found himself in a large valley, at a loch side, with mountains surrounding him. It reminded him of the Great Glen in the highlands of Scotland, but this was a landscape he had never seen before. The waters of the loch were still, and there was no sound. Then came a rushing wind, and he was approached by a giant lion, who was wearing the headdress of a Lakota Chief, full-maned and standing proud, at least as tall as Gunn. Then there followed a goat, a white-horned beast. The lion roared, and the goat cowered. Gunn saw *himself* approach the goat, carrying an axe. He looked down, and saw that he was standing in his own body, yet this *other* version of himself approached the goat. The other Gunn raised the axe, and cleaved off the goat's head. Then the scene faded, and Gunn was aware of his real surroundings, yet he felt no thirst, and no hunger, and a peace that he had not felt in years.

Later, during the closing stage of the ritual, Gunn spoke to Raises Horses about the vision, of the lion and the goat, and the *other* Gunn decapitating the goat.

Raises Horses nodded sagely and spoke, and Joseph translated.

'The *wasicun* Gunn has been granted a gift from Wakan Tanka, a vision of what must be. He must search for the goat, who has defied the ways of Wakan Tanka, and bring death upon him.'

Gunn listened intently to Joseph's translation, and pondered. Then he asked, 'Does the vision guarantee that the goat will be defeated and killed?'

'Nothing is ever certain. The goat has offended Wakan Tanka. The harmony might not be restored, but if the goat is allowed to continue on his path of evil, then the harmony cannot return to these places. Gunn has been chosen by Wakan Tanka to find the goat, and try to kill it. He may not succeed, but this is his path.'

Gunn didn't speak for some time. Then he said, 'The

Great Spirit Wakan Tanka has shown me the way. I will do this.'

As Joseph translated, Raises Horses smiled, and nodded.

Raises Horses led Gunn down from the hilltop, and the rest of the party followed.

The party feasted, and Gunn joined in greedily, because he realized that he was famished.

He asked Brendan, 'How long was I in the ritual?'

'Two days,' his nephew replied.

'*Two days*? It only seemed about four or five hours.'

'Mine was similar, it lasted about three days.'

'I thought Raises Horses said no *wasicun* had ever done it before.'

'They don't see me as *wasicun*. I think they only let you participate in the ritual because you're my uncle. And Raises Horses likes you. Did you understand what you saw?'

'I think so. The lion in the headdress has to be a representation of God. That's God or Wakan Tanka telling me that He exists. Of course, it could all be a hallucination. The fasting and the concentrated prayer create a waking dream. . . .'

'But you don't really think so, do you?'

'No. When the vision ended, I felt a sense of peace that I've not felt for a long time, if ever.'

'And the goat? Do you think that represents White Hat?'

'It had his eyes.'

'And the vision showed you cutting his head off. What are you going to do?'

'I'm going to leave this reservation and find that man.'

'And then?'

'And then I'm going to tell him that God forgives him. And I'm going to take a gun, and shoot him dead.'

CHAPTER FIVE

Gunn set out to find the white-hatted murderer, with Joseph and Brendan travelling with him. The chief allowed them horses and supplies, and they began to tour the western territories. Gunn preached in remote towns and settlements, and there was a meagre living to be made in those places. Sometimes though, there was a rich bounty when the townsfolk realized that they had a man of the cloth come to give them a dose of religion. Courting couples lined up to ask Gunn to marry them, and he was happy to oblige. For a fee, of course.

When they had earned enough money, they bought western-style clothing for Brendan and Joseph, so that they wouldn't face awkward questioning about why the boys looked like Indians.

Everywhere they went, they made discreet enquiries about a large man in a white Stetson, who had maybe four or five associates, but nobody seemed to know of these men. It would be three long years before they got a lead on White Hat.

'God moves in mysterious ways,' Gunn orated.

He paused briefly. He spoke more slowly than he would

in conversation, because of his thick Scottish burr. He looked out at the assembled congregation, and tried to gauge how far he could shock them with this sermon.

Then he spoke again. 'You'll have heard that before, no doubt. I've certainly heard it many times. I've said it many times, usually when I didn't have the slightest idea what God was playing at.'

There was nervous laughter here and there. They had never heard a clergyman speak this way before, Gunn was sure.

'But what does it really mean? God gives you something that you didn't expect. He definitely gave me something that I didn't expect. He killed my wife and my child.'

Gasps. Women tutting. He'd had this reaction before, in other towns.

'Mysterious ways, indeed. How could God do this, to one of his ministers? I never believed it. I thought it must be some kind of joke. I turned from Him, and took up sinful ways. But after a while, I was reminded of the Book of Job. Now Job was just an ordinary guy, no trouble to anybody, God-fearing and decent. But according to the Bible, God and the Devil had a bet. The Devil wagered that if everything went wrong for Job, Job would turn away from God.

'So God let Satan heap punishments on Job. Do you call that fair? Is that justice?'

Gunn paused again.

'What would you do,' he went on, 'if everything started to go wrong for you? Would you blame God, and turn away from him? I know I did. And I'm an ordained minister. How much harder must it be for people who are just trying to live as best they can, and yet troubles seem to come their way? You're just about to harvest your crops, when a cyclone comes across the plain and blows it all away, and maybe blows the roof off the house you built with your bare hands. Perhaps you're a rancher, and a drought lasts for months and most of your herd die of thirst.

'What do you say to God then? Do you say, "Thank you God, for teaching me a lesson, and I promise that I'll be more humble in future." I'll bet you don't. You ask yourself why this should happen to you, when all you want is to provide a future for your family.

'I'd like to tell you that God has a plan for you. That your life will work out. That if you pray, and read the Bible, then God will smooth the path for you and make everything work out for you. But the world isn't like that.

'You have to make your own way in this world.

'You have to live your life as if God didn't exist. Now I'm convinced that God does exist, and that his son Jesus Christ is my – and your – saviour. But there are two different kinds of believers in God. They're called "theists" and "deists". Theists believe that God is watching, knowing everything, and will intervene to help in times of trouble. But that doesn't seem to happen. So where is God? The deists have an answer. They say that God made the world, then decided to take the day off. Forever. God is gone, they say, and isn't coming back. Forget about divine intervention. "You're on your own, laddie," as my Highland grandfather used to say. The only intervening that you'll get is your own, made by the sweat of your brow, the effort of your muscles, and the barrel of a gun.'

The congregation were hushed now. Some of the women at the back, prim and proper, were appalled at what they were hearing, and some of them were rising to leave.

Gunn went on: 'And our Saviour Jesus Christ, he isn't going to intervene to make your life easier. No. He died on the cross at Calvary so that your sins could be washed away, so that you could have eternal life. But only after you're dead. He came back from the dead, so the Bible tells us, just a few days later, to prove that death wasn't the end. But he went off shortly after that, and hasn't been seen since, as far as anybody knows. He promised to come back, and his disciples expected him to return soon, but that was more than nineteen hundred years ago.

'Well, I have to tell you that Jesus isn't coming. And you have to live your life in that knowledge. Life is a struggle, and you have to make your own way. Nobody is coming to save you, to make your path easier. If God has a plan for your life, He isn't telling you what it is. You have to make your plan for yourself. When obstacles get in the way, deal with them as best you can. I learned that the hard way, trying to blot out the pain of my misfortunes. It was only when I realized that I had to stop feeling sorry for myself that I began to find some kind of peace.'

Gunn knew that he couldn't tell them about the Vision Quest. The congregation would lynch him.

'And you have to do the same. God will reward you in heaven. But don't think that He guarantees to reward you in this life. This world is a vale of tears, but that's no reason to bewail your fate. Live as decently as you can, help others less fortunate than you when you can. Christ told you to do that. It's there in the Bible.

'You don't have to turn the other cheek. Do that and the bandits and bullies will just take advantage of you. If some sinner wants to be about the Devil's business, you don't have to let him impose that business on you. Love God, and keep a loaded revolver.

'That's all I have to say just now. Amen.'

Gunn stopped and surveyed the congregation. Some of them were smiling, mainly the ranch hands who had expected that the sermon would be dull and dreary, because of previous preachers they had heard. Others, who had a more convinced view of religion, were glowering at him. He knew what most people in these western territories expected of a minister of the Christian religion. They wanted to hear about gentle Jesus, meek and mild, but Gunn could not teach that any more. Nor could he give them the hellfire and damnation of the Old Testament.

He knew that sometimes there was trouble when he preached this sermon, or variants of it. He had to judge whether it was time to get Brendan to go round with his hat to take up the collection, or to sneak round to the horses to get ready to make a quick getaway. More than once there had been men (and once a woman) who wanted to fight him. He tried to avoid fighting, not because he was afraid of being hit, but he was more afraid of the trouble that would be caused by winning the fight. More than once he'd had to talk his way out of being locked up by the sheriff. He tried to befriend the local law before making his sermons, but that depended on how honest they were. He'd once had to pay the entirety of a collection as a fine in order to stay out of jail.

But some congregations were appreciative of what he had to say, particularly those who believed in hard work and self-reliance. Two different towns had invited him to be their minister, and he had been tempted when one town in New Mexico had offered to convert to the Church of Scotland.

Later, in the saloon, accepting drinks from the ranch hands who had liked his sermon, Gunn asked discreetly about White Hat. As so many times on this quest, nobody knew anything of him.

Gunn and his two companions were settled into a routine. They would ride between towns, Gunn would preach where a congregation was willing to listen, or marry couples in need of marrying, and sometimes officiate at a funeral.

One day, Joseph started to hang back. Normally, Gunn rode out in front, and Brendan and Joseph followed close behind. Joseph started lagging, and after ten minutes of this, Brendan rode up to his uncle and told him that his brother was almost half a mile back. Gunn agreed to halt, and they waited for Joseph to catch up.

When he finally rode up to them a few minutes later, Gunn said, 'What's up, Joseph?'

'We're being followed.'

'Are ye sure, laddie?'

Joseph scoffed. 'Of course I'm sure.'

'Joseph can track anything,' Brendan said, 'and nobody can track him without being noticed.'

'I don't doubt it, Brendan. How many do you think, Joseph?'

'Just a lone rider, Guthrie. Shouldn't be any trouble.'

'How far behind?'

'Not that far. I think he's been following us since the last town.'

'OK, ma boys. Let him catch up with us, if it's only one man.'

There was a low mound up ahead and they went to ground there, so that they couldn't immediately be seen on the trail. They waited a few minutes and a black man rode past them, on a grey mount.

'Hold it right there, mister!' Gunn shouted.

Joseph had an arrow nocked in his bow, and was aiming at the horseman.

The man looked around, saw Gunn and the boys. He swung his right leg backwards over his saddle, remaining in full view of Gunn, and stepped slowly down from his horse.

Turning to face Gunn, he put both hands in the air and stepped slowly towards them. 'I just want to talk to you. The three of you.'

'Do ye know us, then?'

'You're Reverend Gunn, and the young man beside you is your nephew, Brendan Brennan. The lad aiming the arrow at my heart is his . . . well . . . blood brother, I think. I'm not sure what his name is, but I know that you call him Joseph.'

Joseph said, 'It's my name, one of them anyway.'

'Why do ye want to talk to us?'

'I want to help you.'

'And what makes ye think we're in need of help.'

'You're looking for a big fat man wears a white hat.'

Gunn said, 'That's no secret. What do you know of that man?'

'I used to be one of his gang.'

Joseph said, 'I recognize him, Guthrie. He's the black man who held the horses, while the rest of the gang attacked the hunting party. He's the man who put me in the sack.'

Joseph tautened his bow, but Gunn saw the action and motioned for the young man not to loose the arrow.

'And me too, I'll be bound,' Gunn said. 'Is it your habit of putting people in sacks and cutting them with knives.'

'Sorry about that,' the man said. 'It was the only way I could save you from death. I had to cut you, because without blood on my knife, Swiggard wouldn't have believed that I'd killed you.'

'Swiggard?' Gunn said.

'That's his name.'

'And what might yours be?'

'Cal. Caleb Cannon.'

'Well, Mr Cannon. Suppose you tell us what your connection with Swiggard is, and why you've been following us.'

'I want to help you.'

'Why? And how did you know how to find us?'

'I came across you by chance. I was unwell for weeks after Savage shot me. . . .'

'Savage?' Gunn interjected.

'Another man in the gang.'

'Why did he shoot you?'

'Swiggard's orders. Savage told Swiggard that I had betrayed them.'

'Had you?'

'I suppose so. I certainly regretted ever joining their gang.'

'Where are they now?'

'They're the law enforcement, if you could call it that, in a town in Montana. Misery, it's called.'

'Apt name, if White Hat is the law there.'

'Not really. The town was founded by Catholics, they called it Misericordia.'

'Latin for Mercy,' the Scotsman said. 'Can't be much mercy there currently.'

'Swiggard's the sheriff there. I was one of his deputies. I sometimes think I'd be better off if the Confederacy had won and I'd stayed a slave.'

'Why are you not still with him?' Gunn asked.

'He took against me. He fired me. He wanted Randall Savage to kill me, but although Savage shot me, I got away. I'm pretty sure they think I'm dead though.'

He pulled up his shirt, to show the badly stitched up scar in his side.

'Nasty,' Brendan said.

'Savage tried to shoot me in the back, but his aim was a bit off. Lucky for me he'd had too much whiskey the night before. I managed to escape from him, by pretending to fall into the ravine, Savage was too dumb to make sure I was gone. Then I went to some . . . people I know, they patched me up, got me out of the county before Bain and his deputies could discover I wasn't dead.'

'Bain?' Gunn said. 'I thought you said his name was Swiggard.'

'It is,' Cal affirmed. 'But he's going by the name of Nathan Bain.'

Gunn scratched his head. 'Why would that be?'

'Nathan Bain was a man we met one day. He told us he was a war hero, and that he was on his way to Misery to be their sheriff. Showed us a letter from the town, inviting him. Swiggard told Savage to kill him, which he did. Swiggard took the letter, and we went to Misery. Showed the mayor the letter, and passed himself off as Bain, and he's been the sheriff there ever since. He passed his gang off as deputies he'd recruited.'

'Is he a good sheriff?' Brendan asked.

Cal laughed. 'No. He's a mean, swaggering bully. The only real crime in town is committed by him and his deputies. Sadly, me included.'

Joseph said, 'How do we know you can be trusted? Maybe you haven't changed sides.'

Gunn said, 'Now, Joseph, what have I told you about being suspicious?'

'He was part of the gang that killed my people.'

Cal said, 'That's true. I am sorry for that. But I just held the horses. I didn't kill anybody.'

'You put me in a sack, and cut me.'

'Again, guilty on that one. But if I hadn't done that, Swiggard would have ordered Savage to kill you, and *he* would've shot you like a dog.'

Gunn could see that Joseph was relaxing his hold on the arrow in his bow. How difficult must it be for the laddie to stop himself from killing this man, who had been part of the gang that had killed so many people he cared about. But this man hadn't done any of the killing himself, and Gunn and Joseph were alive today because of this man's actions.

'How do ye propose tae help us, then?'

'I can ride along with you, take you in the direction of Misery. I'll have to avoid the town myself, because otherwise Swiggard would get Savage or the others to finish me off. But I can take you there. You should be all right. Perhaps you can pass Joseph off as a Mexican. Dressed the way he is, with that short hair, you'd get away with it.

There's no chance that Swiggard would recognize you, Reverend Gunn. He's so wrapped up in his own fantasies that he barely recognizes anybody, never mind somebody he saw for just a minute or so years ago.'

Gunn thought for a minute, looked across at Brendan and Joseph, then said, 'All right, Mr Cannon. Take us to Misery.'

Joseph added, 'But if you double-cross us, I'll put an arrow through your heart. . . .'

CHAPTER SIX

Gunn was weary, frustrated at the slow progress of the journey from Oregon where Cal had found them, to their destination in Montana. But he knew that after many days of travelling, they were almost there. By Cal's reckoning, Misery was less than a day's ride away.

As they rode along the trail, they saw something up ahead. A wagon had overturned.

Joseph said, 'I'll scout ahead, see if there's any danger.'

He rode off at a gallop towards the wagon, and Brendan followed close behind. Within a minute, they were at the scene. Gunn kept his mount at a slow trot, eyes wary.

Moments later, Joseph rode back to him. 'It's all right, Guthrie. It's just an accident. A wagon's turned over, and the driver's hurt.'

'Let's help the man, ma laddies.' Gunn spurred his horse gently, and they galloped towards the scene, Cal following on behind.

As they got there, Joseph jumped down from his roan. Gunn got down from the saddle more sedately, as befitted a man of his mature years. Joseph hitched both of their horses to one of the wheels of the overturned wagon, where Brendan's mount was already secured. Cal tied his mount and examined the overturned wagon, while Brendan crouched over the injured driver, offering him some water from his canteen.

'You seem to be in some difficulty, sir,' Gunn said.

'You could say that,' the man said. 'I think my ankle's busted.'

'Let me have a look,' Gunn said, kneeling down beside Brendan, and gingerly taking hold of the man's right foot.

The man said, 'Are you a doctor, sir?'

'I have a doctorate. Unfortunately for you, it's in divinity, not medicine.'

'Saints preserve us from God-botherers,' the man said, and chuckled, but winced in pain as he did so.

'I find that usually it's God who bothers me,' Gunn said. 'Not the other way round.'

'Are you a Scotsman?' the man said.

'Aye, sir, that I am. Reverend Doctor Guthrie Gunn, at your service.'

'I'm Chase Hardin. I'm the owner of the Lazy H ranch.'

'Is it near?' Gunn asked.

'We're on its border just now. The ranch house is about five miles further east.'

'Well, Mr Hardin, I'm no medical man, but I think you might have a broken ankle.'

'Damn. That's all I need. Beg your pardon, Reverend, for the profanity.'

'I'd curse too if I got injured, and take the Lord's name in vain for good measure.'

Hardin chuckled, although it hurt.

'The laddie who offered you some water is my nephew,

Brendan Brennan, and the other young man is Joseph, his brother.'

Hardin looked over at Joseph. 'But isn't he. . . ?'

'Aye. It's a long story.'

Hardin looked over at the other figure, who seemed to be hiding behind the overturned wagon. Then he looked more closely when he realized that he recognized the face.

'Caleb Cannon!' Hardin said. 'I thought you'd run away from Bain.'

'No, sir,' the black man said. 'He tried to have me killed. Savage shot me, but didn't quite manage to eliminate me.'

'Why have you come back?'

'I'm travelling with these gentlemen just now. I think they might have some stories to tell you that'll you'll find of interest.'

Hardin gave Gunn a quizzical look, and the Scotsman shrugged. Then Gunn turned to Joseph. 'What do you reckon, laddie. Is the wagon damaged?'

'Not much, Guthrie,' Joseph said. 'It's just toppled over. I think we can right it, the four of us. Just needs a bit of leverage.'

'Fine. Mr Hardin, we'll get your wagon upright, and we can drive you to your home. Can you get medical attention there?'

'One of the hands can fetch a doctor.'

'Sounds like a plan to me,' Gunn said. 'Right, my laddies, let's get to it.'

Gunn and his three companions seized the side of the wagon and pushed. At first it wouldn't move, but all four of them were fit and muscular, and after some effort the wagon was righted. The horses still attached to the wagon were startled that they were suddenly free to move, and made to advance along the trail. But Cal jumped aboard and pulled on the brake.

Joseph and Brendan set to picking up the cargo that had spilt, some of which was undamaged, while Cal checked the horses for injury. Gunn got Hardin to his feet, and supported him as he hobbled over to the wagon. Brendan unhitched their horses and then tethered his uncle's horse to the side of the wagon. Gunn helped Hardin up onto the driver's bench, then joined him there, taking up the reins and loosening the brake.

Gunn drove along the trail, with the others following on horseback. Hardin directed Gunn to the turning that led off towards his ranch house, and they were there less than an hour after righting the wagon.

When they got there, Hardin gave orders to one of his ranch hands to ride to the town of Barstow. Gunn wondered why they didn't send to Misery, which was nearer, but Hardin said he had his own reasons for not having much to do with the place.

Mrs Hardin was concerned to see that her husband had been injured, but he told her not to fuss. He introduced her to his rescuers, and she welcomed them all into the ranch house. She appeared not to know Cal; Gunn mused that it was possible she'd never met him before.

'You fine gentlemen must be hungry,' she said.

'Yes, ma'am,' Brendan said. 'We haven't had anything to eat since early morning.'

'Then let me get something for you.' She headed off to the kitchen.

While they were waiting, Hardin asked them what brought them to these parts.

'We're searching for a man,' Gunn said. 'We understand that he currently goes by the name of Nathan Bain.'

'The sheriff? My daughter's married to him.'

'I'm really sorry to hear that,' Gunn said. 'He's an evil man. At least three of us have very good reasons for wanting him to be dead.'

'And you a man of the cloth too,' Hardin said.

'Doesn't stop me being a man. Doesn't stop me wanting to do what's right.'

'Well,' Hardin said, 'I've no love for Bain. I'd prefer it if he was no longer in the world. But my daughter and granddaughter. . . .'

'If our presence here is troubling to you . . .' Gunn began.

Hardin interrupted. 'Not at all. I won't act against Bain. But he and his cohorts need to be taken down a peg or two. I'll help you, as a sort of sleeping partner.'

'Not much you can do if your leg's busted,' Brendan said.

'I don't know about that. If you're plotting against Bain, it wouldn't be a good idea to base yourselves in town. He's turned it into his own personal fiefdom, and he owns half the businesses, and those he doesn't own he keeps ground down with high levels of taxation, which he and his deputies collect at gunpoint.'

Hardin gave Cal a hard stare, and the black man looked down at his feet, unable to look at Hardin, who remembered him from when he was one of those deputies.

'And your daughter married this man?' Gunn shook his head.

'Even if I do say so myself, she's the handsomest young lady in the county. He set his cap at her, courted her, and also intimidated any other potential suitors. Chased two of them out of town, and another met with an unfortunate accident when cleaning his gun. . . .'

'Hmm,' Gunn said.

'And he can be very charming with the ladies, if he likes the look of them. Everybody else, he treats like dirt. And I've heard tell that when he loses interest in a lady, he treats her as badly as anybody else.'

'Has he done that to your daughter?' Gunn asked.

'Not yet, as far as I know. She visits us quite often. My wife won't allow *him* in the house. But Emmeline looks fine, and Clemmy – that's Clementine, my granddaughter – seems happy and well cared for.'

'But you won't stop us acting against him?'

'Mr Gunn, I'll do everything in my power to help you. Why don't you stay here at the ranch?'

'No, we couldn't presume. . . .'

'I insist. If it was up to me, I'd accommodate you here in the house, but I have an idea that would give you a cover story for being in these parts.'

'Oh?' Gunn said.

'I'll take you on as temporary hands. Yes, that would be the way to do it. Cattle drive is coming up. With my leg, I won't be able to go, but my foreman can take care of it. We need to keep a few hands to work the ranch, and we could use some extra bodies. No room in the bunkhouse, though. I can't put you in the house, because the hands would notice that, and gossip would get out in the town. But until the cattle drive starts, you could bunk in the hayloft.'

'I've slept in worse places,' Gunn said.

'You and your lads could help around the horse corral,

and there are always repairs of one kind or another needing done.'

'Well, I did a bit of carpentry when I was young,' Gunn said, 'before I went into the ministry.'

'That's great,' Hardin said. 'There's always something needs fixing. I won't work you too hard.'

'Then we'll accept your kind offer.'

'We'll move you into the barn just as soon as we can. I'd suggest that your boy Joseph doesn't go into town much. Bain wouldn't like the colour of his skin.'

Gunn said, 'And Cal can't go there, because he's certain to be recognized.'

'Cal, you'd best stay on the ranch,' Hardin said. 'In fact, you'd best stay in the house until the cattle drive. We could pass you off as a new house servant. I don't think that any of the hands would even look at you. Some of them might remember you from the town. . . .'

Just then Mrs Hardin came back with a trolley heaped with sandwiches and a coffee pot. Hardin stopped talking about their plans, and Gunn realized that he didn't want to discuss them in front of his wife. After he said a somewhat perfunctory grace, he and the boys ate.

CHAPTER SEVEN

Chase Hardin sat resting on the veranda in the late afternoon sunshine, but looked up when he heard a buggy coming over the ridge. He wasn't expecting visitors, so he kept a close eye on it, relaxing when he recognized his daughter.

Emmeline Hardin Bain was slim, with long blonde hair. She looked too young to be a married woman with a three-year-old daughter, but she was in fact in her mid-twenties. She had almond-shaped eyes, an almost-dazzling blue, with a pointed chin and high cheekbones. All the men stared at her whenever she walked by, and she could have had her pick of any man in the territory, yet somehow the unprepossessing sheriff had seduced her and married her.

Chase got up and went to meet her, limping slightly. Emmeline climbed down from the buggy, went around the horses, patting their necks as she passed them, and went around to the other side of the wagon, reaching up to lift down her daughter.

The child rushed to greet her grandfather. He grabbed her in his arms and raised her up, then looked at his daughter quizzically.

'Emmy, what brings you here today?' Emmy gave him a frown. 'Not that we're not pleased to see you. . . .'

As she approached him, he saw that she had a black eye.

'Has that man been hitting you? Again?'

'No, Papa. I just had an accident.'

'You accidentally bumped against Bain's fist, you mean?'

'No, Papa.'

'One thing I can't stand, a man who hits a woman. I've a good mind to ride into town. . . .'

'No. Don't do that.'

'Why not?'

'I've left him.'

'Not before time. What did he do to you?'

'I don't want to talk about that.'

Emmeline told Clemmy to go indoors and see her grandmother. She hoped that this would distract her mother from asking why they were here. Bain was never invited to the Lazy H because her parents could not stand him.

'Well,' Hardin said. 'I'm glad to see you'

Emmeline frowned. 'It's good to be home. I've put up with that man for longer than I should have.'

Chase said, 'Should we take precautions here, in case he tries to take you back by force?'

Emmy shook her head. 'I don't think that there's any need. He probably won't even notice that I'm gone.'

'Well, I can't say that I'm sorry that you've left him. Why don't you take Clemmy in to see her granny, and we'll talk later.'

Emmy nodded, and took the child indoors. As they

went, Hardin reflected that now that Emmy was no longer with that ghastly man, he could help Gunn and the others to act against him with more than just moral support.

He found it hard to suppress a grin at the thought. *Good,* he thought. *Bain, or Swiggard – whatever his name is – will get what's coming to him at last.*

Swiggard sat in the office, pretending to do paperwork. In his mind, he was no longer Swiggard, having managed to convince himself that he was Nathan Bain, that he had always been Nathan Bain, and that there had never been a person named Mark Swiggard.

It had seemed so good a town when he had first arrived. Most of the people of the county had been so grateful that such a great man had consented to be their sheriff. The rumours that reached him, via Bick Billson and Harry Watney, his deputies, that when the time had come for re-election, Mayor Pinkston had wanted another candidate to run against him, well that must have been drunken talk in the saloon, because Bain knew he was so popular that he would win 100 per cent of any ballot. It had been so sad that Pinkston had met an unfortunate accident while cleaning his gun, because had he lived he would have denied any such rumour.

Bain knew that soon he would be looking to move on to better things. He had ambitions, oh yes, great ambitions indeed. This had been a good move, taking this position in Misery. Being a lawman wasn't just about catching criminals and bringing them to justice, oh no. It was about bringing order and discipline to a town and a county. Bain knew all about order and discipline, and he knew how to enforce those, by gunpoint if necessary.

But there would come a time to move on. Maybe not this year, or next. But soon. . . .

The plan was to have a career in politics. Bain had certainly put away enough money in his six years as county sheriff to be able to fund a political campaign. But Cal had suggested that he needed more than just money. He needed something to make him famous, not just in the western territories, but throughout the entire nation. It can't have been Cal who first suggested that he write a book, it must have been Bain himself.

'You're absolutely right,' Cal had said, agreeing with Bain's suggestion. 'You need to write an autobiography.'

Bain had temporarily misheard, for he had asked. 'A not to buy geography? What's that?'

'A book about your life and doings, written by yourself. Of course, a great lawman like you . . . you wouldn't have the time to write it yourself. . . .'

'Wouldn't I?' Bain had asked.

'No. You're certainly capable, being the smartest man in the territory. . . .'

Bain had failed to notice that Cal's nostrils were flaring as he spoke those last words.

'I am that,' Bain had agreed. No doubt about that in the slightest.

Cal, before Bain had fired him, had suggested that they approach a famous author, and that although that writer was only helping a busy lawman to write his book, the fact he was a famous author would show just what a great man Bain truly was. Cal had a nice turn of phrase – pity he turned out to be a traitor. Bain had liked the sound of that. *Great man.* Emmy suggested the names of several authors. William Dean Howells, Herman Melville,

Nathaniel Hawthorne. Bain had never heard of them, and thought that they all sounded like pansies, but Emmy assured him that they were all great writers. She had even suggested Harriet Beecher Stowe. Bain *had* heard of her, he was mightily sick of Emmy going on about that woman. She can't have been as great as they all said. Bain had done more for black people than anybody. He'd employed a black deputy. Just a pity that hadn't worked out so well. . . .

Emmy had tried to contact these scribblers, writing to them to enquire whether they would be interested in corroborating (sounded like that anyway) in the writing of the book. Melville's publisher advised that he was exhausted after having worked on an epic poem about the Holy Land, so could not consider the commission. Bain was relieved that this Melville had turned him down, being quite sure that a poet must be a sissy, and therefore not suitable for *transcraping* (he thought that was the word) the true doings of a real man like Bain. Hawthorne's publishers wrote back that he had unfortunately died in 1864. Bain had laughed at Emmy's *iggerance*, if she'd asked him he could have told her, 'cause he knew all there was to know about such things. She didn't say anything when he told her that.

Bain began to think that it wouldn't be a bad idea to get Mrs Stowe after all. Emmy had told him that she had met President Lincoln, and the president had said that she'd been the woman who'd started the Civil War. Bain doubted this very much – he'd seen no sign of any women on the battlefield – and rebuked Emmy for her annoying chatter.

'Emmy,' he'd said to her, 'what did reading ever get anybody?'

Emmy had just burst into tears, and had gone to stay with her folks for a fortnight. Who can figure women?

Savage still wanted to go through with the plan of getting somebody to write Bain's life story. He showed real support and loyalty.

It was Emmy who introduced Bain to the work of Flint Andrews. Emmy liked to read to him, and he was often too tired after a hard day of enforcing the law to be bothered to argue with her. She liked rubbish by a woman named Austin (or maybe it was Austen), real sissy books about soppy women trying to find rich husbands, and even worse books by some crazy dames named Brunty (he thought that was the name, anyway) where the women were desperate for any kind of man, and liked walking on moors (whatever they might be) in a place called Yorkshire (a phony name if ever he'd heard one). Bain told her he didn't like this kind of rubbish. Emmy knew better than to argue, so she borrowed a dime novel from one of the hands who worked at her father's ranch. Bain thought that a ranch hand who read books must be lazy, and not pulling his weight. If such a man were working for Bain, he'd be fired in no time. Like Cal. . . .

But Bain had liked the book, *Missouri Vengeance*, by some guy named Flint Andrews. Bain was determined that this was the man to help him write his book, and he determined to hire him at any cost.

Of course, it wouldn't really be Flint Andrews writing the story of Nathan Bain, it would be Bain himself, and Andrews would just do the donkey-work of copying down the words. And if there should be any trouble with that arrangement, then Savage could always step in to sort the matter out. Just the way that he'd done with Cal. . . .

Frederick Abernathy arrived in Misery on the noon stage on a bright September day. The stage arrived about half an hour late, which he now knew was reasonable from the experiences that he'd had over the last few days. He stepped down from the coach, relieved that the journey was over, and he was looking forward to meeting Nathan Bain.

He wondered about whether the man himself would be here to meet him.

A young man approached him, barely out of his teens. He looked like some kind of hotel bellboy. Obviously not Nathan Bain.

'Mr Abernathy?'

'I am,' Abernathy said.

'I'm Geoffrey,' the boy said. 'From the hotel. Mr Bain is too busy to meet you in person, so I've been sent. We'll get you settled in the hotel, and Mr Bain will meet you for dinner there this evening.'

'Fair enough. Where is the hotel?'

'It's just down the block, at the corner.'

The shotgun messenger had lifted Abernathy's baggage down onto the boardwalk, and Geoffrey picked it up.

'Lead the way please, Geoffrey,' Abernathy said.

The young man led Abernathy along the boardwalk, past the saloon and the chandler's store. Geoffrey led him across the side street to the hotel, which was located in a block on its own.

Geoffrey pushed at the entrance door with his free hand, and said, 'This way, please.'

He led Abernathy across the lobby to the reception

desk, behind which stood an elegantly dressed mature man, with a thick neatly cut head of grey hair and a thick moustache that still had some red in it, but was speckled with grey.

'Good afternoon, sir,' the clerk said to Abernathy.

Geoffrey said, 'This gentleman is Mr Frederick Abernathy.'

The clerk said, 'Ah, yes, Mr Bain's guest. Welcome, Mr Abernathy. We have our best room reserved for you.'

The clerk turned and reached towards ornate mahogany shelving on the wall behind the desk. Keys were hooked to various cubbyholes. The clerk took the key numbered 24 and held it out for Geoffrey to take.

'Geoffrey will show you to your room. I trust that you will find it satisfactory.' The clerk then added, 'Mr Bain will meet you for dinner in the hotel dining room at 7:30 sharp.'

'Will I get into trouble if I'm late?'

The clerk just frowned.

'This way, sir,' Geoffrey said, picking up the bag again. He led Abernathy to a grand staircase, and they climbed to the floor above.

Geoffrey conducted him to Room 24. The room was well-appointed, large and airy, with a big bay window that gave a good view of the street below. Geoffrey laid the bags down at the foot of an imposing four-poster bed. This was much more luxury than Abernathy was used to. Often short of money, he was unable to patronise establishments as grand as this back East.

Geoffrey handed the door key to Abernathy, and said, 'Will there be anything else, sir?'

Abernathy slipped his hand into his jacket pocket, and

slipped out a half-dollar coin, and proffered it to Geoffrey, who shook his head.

'No, sir. Normally I would accept a gratuity from a guest, but we're under orders that you are Mr Bain's guest, and that he will reward us appropriately if he considers that our service to you is of a decent standard.'

Abernathy held out the coin. 'Go on, Geoffrey. Take it. This is from the expenses money that Mr Bain sent me, so it's really coming from him.'

Geoffrey looked uncertain.

Abernathy said, 'I won't tell if you won't.'

Geoffrey smiled and held out his hand. Abernathy dropped the coin into it, and Geoffrey pocketed it swiftly.

'Thank you very much, sir. If there's anything that I can do for you, anything at all. . . .'

'As a matter of fact,' Abernathy said, 'I was wondering if there might be a possibility of something to eat.'

'Yes, sir. The dining room is serving luncheon, and your needs can be taken care of there. And since you are Mr Bain's guest, he will pay for it.'

'And where is the dining room?'

'Just downstairs, through a doorway behind the staircase. Would you like to freshen up first?'

'I would indeed.'

'Well I'll nip down to the kitchen and let them know to expect you in a few minutes.'

'Good man, Geoffrey.'

Abernathy took Geoffrey by surprise by shaking his hand. This was not the customary etiquette between staff and guests. But Geoffrey didn't flinch from the handshake, and returned it firmly as an equal.

Then he left Abernathy alone in the room.

*

After lunch, Abernathy returned to his room and sat watching the town through the bay window.

He watched the townspeople walking along the board-walks, sometimes entering a shop like the mercantile or the chandler, and saw unshaven men make their way into the barber shop, and clean-shaven men leaving. He saw wagons pulled by horses setting off with their supplies, heading out of town.

Even if the Bain project turned sour, he would have gained enough material to write twenty or thirty new dime novels.

He looked across to the sheriff's office, where he could see Bain standing outside talking to some deputies. Tall and stocky, in fact tending to obesity, the man towered over the others. His white Stetson gleamed in the after-noon sunlight, with a golden-coloured hat band. It was a different style of hat from the standard black Stetsons that the deputies wore, having a stiffer brim and a rounder crown, the style known as 'Boss of the Plains'. Bain also wore a brilliantly white vest, which sported a tin star much larger than was usual. The man had very distinctive pierc-ing blue eyes, a chubby face with a crooked nose that had clearly been broken some years earlier, and a lop-sided grin that made him look benevolent. Although, as Abernathy watched the sheriff as he talked with a deputy, his eyes narrowed and his smile turned into a grotesque grimace, suggesting depths of anger that his normally affable demeanour would usually conceal.

Not quite what Abernathy had imagined. Could this really be the war hero that he had learned about when he visited West Point to research the man's military record? Several years had gone by, so the man could have gained weight. Who was Abernathy to judge? Perhaps the man would turn out to be the epitome of the hero of the west. Time would tell.

Abernathy came down from his room a little before 7:30. He approached the dining room doorway, and paused. There were a few diners there already, but he didn't see his host. A waiter approached him, and said, 'This way, please, Mr Abernathy.'

He followed to an alcoved section secluded from other diners. The table set there had two place settings, one already occupied by his host.

Bain rose, surprisingly dainty for such a large man, and extended his hand to Abernathy.

'Mr Arbuthnot,' he said, 'delighted to meet yuh.'

Abernathy took the man's hand, a great paw that enclosed his own, and made no reaction to the use of the wrong name.

'Why don't you call me Flint Andrews?' Abernathy said. 'After all, it's his writing talents you're employing, not mine.'

Bain looked puzzled, then smiled, just his mouth, with no change in his unfocused, watery eyes. He peered at Abernathy as if he needed eyeglasses but was too vain to wear them.

'Right you are, Mr Andrews. I see what yuh did there. Mah deputy tole me that Andrews warn't your real name, but I guess he wuz wrong.'

'It depends on how you look at it, I suppose,' Abernathy said.

The sheriff looked blank. 'Whatever yuh say, Flinty boy. Whatever yuh say.'

Abernathy couldn't think of anything to add, so didn't. Bain signalled with a nod, and the waiter headed through the door to the kitchen. Wasn't the man going to take their order? Come to think of it, Abernathy hadn't been provided with a menu.

The waiter brought a beef broth, setting the first plate in front of Abernathy, and then the other was placed before Bain.

'I took the *liberal* of ordering for us in advance,' Bain said, 'so that we don't have to wait while the chef cooks it. I hate waiting.'

Abernathy noted silently that Bain did not have the courtesy to find out whether his guest wanted what was ordered for him.

Bain slurped at the broth, and spoke as he did so. 'Great to have yuh here to assist the writing of my autobiol – autoliebog – .'

Abernathy said, 'Autobiography. Or memoirs, if you prefer.'

Bain frowned. '*Mem-worse?* Don't sound right tuh me.'

'It's French.'

'Then can't be right. Mah book's going tuh be in plain American.'

Abernathy thought, *Is this guy for real?* Some kind of hick act, making out that he's as dumb as a hitching post, so that the war hero and esteemed lawman would seem 'jest folks'?

'Well, anyhoo,' Bain said. 'This is how it's going tuh work. I don't have that much time tuh spare, being a law officer and all, so yuh'll meet with me mornings, three

75

times a week. Yuh'll come tuh my home, nine sharp in the morning. One my deputies, maybe Bick Billson or Harry Watney, will call for yuh at half past eight in the morning here at the hotel tomorrow, and he'll bring yuh the first time.'

Bain had finished his broth, although Abernathy had barely started on his. Bain nodded to the waiter, who hurried off, and brought back a second bowl.

'Being sheriff makes for a hearty appetite. Eat up now, Flinty boy. That stuff'll put hairs on your chest.'

Abernathy already had hairs on his chest.

Bain finished his seconds while Abernathy had barely taken half of his firsts.

'Eat up, man. There's a prime steak waiting for us in the kitchen, and while I like it well-done, I don't need it burnt tuh cylinders.'

Abernathy said, 'Why don't you get the waiter to bring the main course? I'll be ready by the time it gets here.'

Bain nodded to the waiter, who made his way back to the kitchen. He returned with two large plates, heaped with sirloin steak, potatoes, peas and gravy.

'No wonder yuh so skinny, Flinty boy, yuh hardly take enough in yuh tuh keep a mouse alive.'

Abernathy picked at his steak. It was too much for him, but he made an effort, not wanting to antagonize Bain. The man talked like a buffoon, but he must be capable. He'd have lost his position in the county if he was as idiotic as he seemed. Wouldn't he?

Oh, well, he would meet with Bain, hear his story. If nothing else, there was bound to be material for future dime novels. But perhaps that was all he would get. There was definitely something screwy about this set-up. He didn't know what yet, but he was sure that he would find out.

CHAPTER EIGHT

Gunn sat alone at a table in the back of the saloon, trying to be inconspicuous, sipping the spirituous liquor that was at least wet and alcoholic, even if it wasn't a 20-year-old single malt, and he fretted. He wasn't sure if he wanted to become a killer. There were those commandments, those troublesome instructions that Moses had brought down from Mount Sinai. He was comfortable with some of them. Honour thy father and thy mother. No difficulty with that. No other Gods but me. Well, Wakan Tanka undoubtedly is God, Gunn was convinced of that. Just because the Lakota had a different name for the Supreme Being, and a different theology, that didn't mean it wasn't the same God. But 'Thou Shalt Not Kill'? He was having trouble with that one. Not kill? Not ever? What about in self-defence? What about in war? When you're sent into battle, are you to let the other guy kill you just because he's a sinner who doesn't believe in following the commandments?

In any case, Gunn was a Christian rather than a Hebrew. Some of the really fevered preachers he knew, real fanatical Presbyterians – much like he had been when he was a parish minister in Scotland – they preferred the

Old Testament to the New Testament, presumably because the God they were preaching about was vengeful, smiting enemies and sending sinners to hell. It was great stuff, especially when the sinners being sent to eternal damnation were your enemies. But it was as if these people didn't believe in Christ's message at all. Christ only had two commandments. Love your God with all your mind and all your soul; that was the first of them. Not difficult, that one, because God made the universe, so it's easy to be thankful for that. Without the universe, you wouldn't be existing to do the loving. But the other commandment, that was harder. Love one another. *Love one another?* What did that mean? Love your wife or your children. Easy, Gunn knew. Love your next-door neighbour? Not like you love your family, but you can still have a high regard for him. But your enemy? The man who's done you wrong? Not so simple. Gunn had struggled to love God when he'd blamed him for taking away his wife and child. How could Gunn love Swiggard, who'd murdered his sister and her husband and daughter, never mind all his other crimes? Swiggard's only commandment must have been *Thou shalt kill. And steal. And lie and cheat.* As often as possible.

Gunn hated Swiggard, hated him with the same ferocity that he loved God and Christ. Was he still expected to include him in the 'one another' in 'Love one another'? Perhaps Christ, without any sin at all, could love Swiggard. But what kind of cockamamie religion expected you to love a loathsome creature like the man calling himself Bain?

He wanted to blow Swiggard's brains out. He wanted to take an axe to his throat and chop his head off. A man of such evil didn't deserve to live, did he? But . . . Thou shalt not kill. Gunn pondered. Maybe thou shalt, he thought. He wasn't sure what was the right thing to do.

Abernathy pushed his way through the batwings of the saloon. He knew that this was a place where he could get some escape from Bain. The man was impossible. Bain lied about almost everything, even things that were easily provable. He claimed to be six feet six inches tall, but Abernathy could see that he was only two inches taller than his own six feet. He bragged that he weighed two hundred and fifty pounds, but Abernathy thought it was obvious from the man's girth that he was well over three hundred pounds. His ridiculous claims that he was good at everything were not borne out by any evidence. Testimony from the townsfolk, yes, about what a great sheriff they had, oh yes, and all of them had the same nod of the head as they said it, but there was no actual proof that Bain had a talent for anything other than shouting at people, and making dumb remarks. Abernathy thought that the townsfolk had a vacancy in their eyes when they talked of Nathan Bain, as if they were reciting by rote something they'd had to learn.

The interview sessions had become something to dread. He pretended to take notes in shorthand, but wrote gibberish. His trick memory allowed him to remember everything that was said to him, so he really didn't need to write it down in order to be able to remember it.

He knew that Bain wouldn't make an appearance in the saloon. One of the few boasts that Bain made that was true was that he didn't drink alcohol. So Abernathy knew that he could have a whiskey or two here without being bothered. The deputies might look in from time to time, but they would leave him alone.

He requested a whiskey from the bartender, and looked around to see if there was a quiet table where he could sit without being bothered. There were no vacant tables, but there was one towards the rear of the saloon that was less rowdy than some of the others. There were two wild groups whooping it up tonight, some of the hands from the Lazy H, Chase Hardin's ranch, and the other was a rough-looking group of mountain men. He was sure that they would be interesting fellows, full of stories that he could use for his novels, but he really didn't feel like making the attempt tonight.

Abernathy went to the quietest table, where sat an odd-looking fellow he had seen about the town a few times.

'Do you mind if I sit here, sir?' Abernathy said.

'Naw, sir. Don't mind at all.'

'That's an interesting accent. Scottish, isn't it?'

'It is that. Most people in this country think I'm Irish.'

'I've met Scots before, in New York. I like them, mostly.'

The writer offered his hand to the Scotsman, who accepted it and shook it firmly.

'Name's Abernathy, Frederick Abernathy. I'm a writer.'

'I'm the Reverend Doctor Guthrie Gunn.'

'A clergyman?'

'Indeed. The Church of Scotland.'

'A Presbyterian. Better not refer to you as "Father" then.'

'Quite right, laddie. And not "Vicar" either.'

'Doctor of Divinity?'

'I'm impressed. I normally have to explain to people that I cannae fix up their wounds or give them a potion to help their lumbago. I was awarded my Doctorate by the

University of Glasgow in 1852.'

'What brings you to Misery?'

'Somebody told me this was where I could find the man who murdered my sister. I intend to convert him.'

'To Christianity?'

'Naw. To death.'

'Have you found this man?'

'Aye.'

Abernathy gave the Reverend a quizzical look.

Gunn said, 'That means "yes". I sometimes revert to my mither tongue when I've had a dram or two.'

'Dram?' Abernathy said.

'A wee glass of spirituous liquor. Preferably Scotch whisky. But I'm having to make do with this disgusting concoction.' Gunn frowned at the glass in front of him on the table.

'You were saying about the man who murdered your sister, that you've found him.'

'I have indeed.'

'Who is he?'

'The man who calls himself Nathan Bain.'

'The sheriff? I'm meant to be ghost-writing his autobiography.'

'I knew that. Tell me, sir, are you of the Presbyterian persuasion yourself?'

Abernathy said, 'No, I'm not. I have a sceptical view of religion.'

'Quite right. I would too if I weren't on a mission from God.'

'God gave you a mission? Came to you as a vision of a burning bush? Told you to kill Nathan Bain?'

'Something like that. But I know Bain isn't his name.'

'I've been certain there was something phony about him right from the start. How do you know this?'

'He bushwhacked me, some years ago, him and his gang. In Dakota. One of his gang is reformed, and found me and told me about him.'

'I knew it. The swaggering idiot who's been telling me a load of lies couldn't be the war hero that he claims to be. How did he end up pretending to be Nathan Bain?'

'Long story. There's a man you should meet. Name of Cal Cannon. He can tell you all about Mark Swiggard.'

'Is that his name?'

Gunn nodded. 'God told me to kill him, or die trying. I prefer the former option.'

'Forgive me, but you seem like a sane man. Where I come from, when people claim to have talked to God, they get locked up in the lunatic asylum.'

'Quite right, Mr Abernathy. . . .'

'Fred will do.'

'All right, Fred,' the Scotsman said. 'If I heard people say that God had told them to do something, I'd think that they were crazy. But I undertook a Sioux Vision Quest. . . .'

'Interesting,' Abernathy said.

. . . and Wakan Tanka. . . .'

'What's that?'

'The Great Spirit, Lakota equivalent of God. Wakan Tanka gave me a vision in which I saw myself killing a big fat goat wearing a white Stetson. It had Swiggard's eyes. Before the vision I doubted that God existed. Not any more. I set to hunting the fat man.'

'And you found him?'

'It took me more than three years.'

'And you haven't tried to kill him?'

'With his deputies around him, it isn't easy.'

'Do you have a plan?'

'Not really. I'm proficient with a rifle, thanks to time spent hunting game birds and deer in the Highlands of Scotland, and I've been practising with a revolver. My nephew and his brother. . . .

Again, a puzzled frown from Abernathy. 'Don't you mean your two nephews?'

'I'm not related to my nephew's brother. He's a Lakota tribesman.'

'I'm not understanding this at all.'

'Another long story. If you were to come out to Hardin's barn I'd introduce you to them, and they could tell you. Cal Cannon's there, too.'

'You're in Hardin's barn?'

'It's as good a place to sleep as any. Better than some.'

'Hardin is Bain's father-in-law.'

'We know that. Hardin hates him. He's helping us.'

'How did you meet Hardin?'

'Yet another long story.'

'Looks like I'll have to take you up on that invitation. I'm always on the lookout for good stories. I write dime novels.'

'I suppose somebody has to,' quipped the Scotsman. Then he said, 'We could use a spy in the enemy camp.'

'I gladly volunteer.'

'Why don't you come out to Hardin's barn tomorrow, and we can discuss it?'

'Well, I would, but. . . .'

'Is there some problem?' Gunn asked.

'It's just that I don't ride. I can't ride.'

Gunn shook his head, then opened his mouth as if to

make a cutting remark, then changed his mind, and said, 'Well, I suppose Brendan – that's my nephew – could borrow a buggy and come to get you. I'll arrange it.'

Two days later, Abernathy was in the saloon once more.

He'd had his meeting with Gunn and his three companions. He'd got to know Brendan quite well during the drives to and from the ranch, and had been astonished at his extraordinary history. Brendan had been delighted when he offered to use the incidents of his life in his novels. And when he had met Joseph Brennan, alias Red Ghost, alias Kicking Buffalo, he had been even more impressed. As they and Gunn told him their stories, his contempt for Bain (or rather Swiggard) turned into a blazing hatred, and he vowed that he would do all that he could to help them.

Joseph had offered to teach him to ride a horse, and Gunn would help him learn to shoot. He agreed to visit them again, when he could.

Interviewing Bain had become more difficult to bear after he'd learned the truth about him. He had met with him again that morning, and found that he could hardly bear to listen to the man. He was sure that the sheriff would notice. But 'Bain' was lost in a world of his own, believing his own myth, convinced that every lie was the truth, and that *Nathan Bain: American Hero*, as the book was to be titled, would further his political ambitions. Abernathy was writing this book, for the sake of appearances, but he was now also writing another exposing Swiggard for the monster that he truly was.

As Abernathy sipped his whiskey, Gunn came in and approached him.

85

'Good evening, Guthrie,' Abernathy said. 'I wasn't expecting to see you here tonight.'

'Sometimes I just need to be in the company of a grown man. Brendan and Joseph are good laddies, but they're jist boys. They're still under thirty. A man needs company of a more mature kind sometimes.'

'Well, Guthrie, sit down and I'll buy you a drink. I know this stuff they sell isn't up to the standards of Scotch. . . .'

'As long as it can wet ma whistle, it'll do for now.'

Abernathy was about to approach the bar to buy a drink for Gunn when there was a sudden hush in the saloon. Two strangers came abruptly through the batwings. The shorter of them walked up to the bar, with his companion a pace behind.

'Good evening, gentlemen,' Joe the bartender said. 'What can I get you?'

'Well, now,' the man said, 'my brother and I are mighty parched from the trail, and we're looking to quench that thirst.'

'Two whiskeys?' Joe suggested.

'Exactly what I had in mind.'

Joe poured two whiskeys, and placed them in front of the strangers. 'You want the whole bottle?'

The man beamed. 'I like a man who knows exactly what kind of hospitality to offer to strangers.'

He pushed a coin across the counter, and Joe scooped it up. The two men picked up the glasses of whiskey, with the one who had spoken picking up the other glass in his right hand, and taking the bottle in his left. Then they looked around the saloon.

They saw that the only half-empty table was the one at which Abernathy and Gunn were sitting. The man with the bottle approached them.

'I wonder if you gentlemen would mind if my brother and I could sit at this table. We're tired from the trail, and we'd appreciate a chance to rest our weary leg-bones.'

Abernathy glanced at Gunn, who nodded.

Abernathy then said, 'Feel free.'

'Neighbourly of you,' the stranger said, and he and his companion took the empty seats.

'My name's Frederick Abernathy, and this is Mr Gunn. He's working at the Hardin ranch just now, the Lazy H.'

The man carrying the whiskey bottle introduced himself. 'The name's James Jackson, and this is my brother Finn.'

Abernathy said, 'Pleased to meet you both. What brings you to Misery? Just passing through?'

The brother now spoke. 'Something like that. We've been doing some gold prospecting out west, and we've decided to make our way back home.'

'And where's home?'

Finn said, 'Mi—' but his brother interrupted, saying, 'Ohio.'

Abernathy said, 'That's a mighty distance.'

Jackson nodded. 'We've been taking it easy. There's no great hurry to get where we're going. If we like the look of a town, we may stay for a while, even for as long as a week or two.'

'What about you, Mr Abernathy?' Finn asked. 'Why are you here?'

Abernathy said, 'I'm a writer, here working on a project.'

Finn scratched his head. 'Never heard of a writer named Frederick Abernathy.'

Abernathy laughed. 'Not many people have. I did have a novel published years ago, under my own name, but it's long forgotten. Now I write dime novels, but I use a pseudonym.'

'Because you're ashamed to admit to them?' Jackson asked.

'Not at all,' Abernathy said. 'I've written for newspapers under my real name, and that novel. Not as good as anything by Hawthorne or Melville. Or even Mark Twain. But my publishers didn't think my name was rugged enough, so we came up with an alternative.'

'And what was that?'

'Flint Andrews.'

Jackson's steely eyes fixed upon Abernathy's face, as if only now really seeing him for the first time.

'The author of *Missouri Vengeance*?' Jackson said.

'Why, yes. Have you read it?'

'*Read it*? I'm *in* it.'

Abernathy frowned. 'What do you mean?'

'I wasn't quite honest with you before when I told you my name. Like you, I've been using a pseudonym. I'm not James Jackson. My real name's Jesse James.'

CHAPTER NINE

Gunn felt his jaw drop open. Jesse James? The outlaw? Was this man really the notorious bandit?

James held out his hand to Gunn, offering to shake. Gunn hesitated. Then he held out his hand and shook the outlaw's hand firmly.

Abernathy also held out his hand, and the outlaw grasped it and shook vigorously.

'It's an honour to meet you, Mr James,' Abernathy said. 'I've never met a real-life outlaw before.'

'I hope I'm not too much of a disappointment to you,' Jesse said.

'You're really Jesse James?' Gunn asked.

'The one and only. I gather that you've heard of me.'

Gunn nodded.

Gesturing towards his companion, Jesse said, 'Then you may also have heard of my brother, Frank.'

Gunn said, 'I've read about your exploits in the newspapers.'

Abernathy said, 'But what are you doing in Montana? I take it what you told us before about travelling east is all baloney.'

Jesse nodded. 'It is. We were in this territory before, back in '73. I knew of a place in Montana with a lot of former Confederate soldiers, so I figured we would be safe there. We were laying low after a big train robbery we pulled off.

'The sheriff of that county took a liking to us, his name was Charles Warren. He was an all right fella, even though he'd worn dark blue during the War. Pine Lodge County, it was. He told us that as long as we didn't break any Territorial laws, he wouldn't bother us. He was good company.

'You might say we're on the lam again, so we've come back to Montana. We thought we would go back to Pine Lodge and look Warren up again. But it's a long way from Missouri, and we're taking our time.'

'You're not quite what I imagined,' Abernathy said to the brothers.

'You described us pretty well in your book,' Frank said.

'I got your description from a photograph of the two of you I saw in a newspaper. You look older now.'

Jesse said, 'We *are* older now. I know the picture you mean, it was taken years ago. We're even more famous now, thanks to writers like you.'

Abernathy said, 'Did you ever think of taking up a safer profession?'

Jesse said, 'Frank always wanted to be a schoolteacher. . . .'

Frank interrupted. 'True. But the war changed that. The teachers are nearly all women now. For a lot less pay. It seemed a better idea to go into . . . business . . . with my brother.'

'Dangerous business,' Gunn said.

'Makes it more fun, though,' Jesse quipped.

'Rather you than me,' said Gunn. 'The most danger I risk is telling people things they don't want to hear when I'm making a sermon.'

'Gunn?' Jesse said. 'I've heard of you. You're the mad Scotch preacher . . .'

'Now just a minute, laddie. I don't mind you calling me mad. But I'm a Scot or a Scotsman. Not Scotch. That's whisky.'

'Begging your pardon, sir,' Jesse said. 'Never met a Scotsman before.'

'No offence taken. Just don't make the same mistake again. And I'm not one for being called sir.'

'How about padre?' Jesse asked.

'No, definitely not. That's Spanish for "father". Too Popish for my taste. And definitely not "vicar". I hate those Anglicans worse than the Roman lot. My name's Guthrie, don't mind it being shortened to Guthrie.'

'And I'm Jesse.'

'Dear oh dear. Sounds very like the Scots word "jessie".'

'And what's wrong with that?' Jesse asked.

'When we call somebody a big jessie, it means he's weak or effeminate. . . .'

Frank James chuckled.

'Shut up, Frank,' Jesse said.

Gunn went on, 'I know it's a Biblical name. . . .'

Frank said, 'Of course it is. He was the father of King David. . . .'

'Shoulda been a schoolteacher,' Jesse interjected.

Gunn continued, '. . . and the name in Hebrew means "king", or sometimes "God exists". Way the Hebrews said it, it sounds more like "Yeshy". Which sounds a bit like

Yeshua or Joshua, which was Jesus's name before the Christians started mispronouncing it. Do you mind, Mr James, if I call you Joshua.'

'That's fine, Guthrie. What is it that brings you to this town?'

Gunn said, 'That's a long story.'

Abernathy nodded. 'It is at that.'

'The night is yet young,' Jesse said, 'and we like a good story.'

Next morning, Randall Savage came into the sheriff's office.

Bain said, 'Anything tuh report, Rand?'

'Two strangers in town. Checked into the hotel yesterday afternoon, don't like the look of them.'

'Got their names?'

'Two brothers named Jackson. James and Finn.'

'They staying long?'

'Don't know, boss. They tole the hotel clerk that it depends.'

'Any reason to think that they might be trouble?'

'Couldn't say. Their faces seemed familiar. They carried themselves like lawmen. Federal marshals, maybe.'

'Possibly you could get Billson and Watney to pervade them tuh leave town.'

Savage knew better than to tell the boss that the word was 'persuade', not 'pervade'.

'Will do, boss. I'll set them on it this afternoon.'

The morning passed with the regular tax collections from the various businesses in town. Bain and Savage visited all the premises in turn, collecting the taxes. The only premises that didn't have their taxes collected were those that were owned by Bain himself.

The one exception on the visit was the whorehouse.

Unbeknown to the people of the town, Bain was the owner of the whorehouse. He was the man behind the madam, Ellen Breakheart. She acted as if she was the owner, but Bain was the real proprietor, keeping the lion's share of the profits, on which he paid no taxation. Bain always made it the last stop on the taxation round, to 'sample the merchandise'. Savage had often heard Bain brag that he was a one-woman man. Sure he was, one woman at a time.

As Bain entered the brothel, Savage went back to the sheriff's office to mind the store.

Billson and Watney turned up at noon.

Savage said, 'The sheriff has a task for you. Two strangers, need to move them on.'

'Where are they?' Billson asked.

'In the hotel.'

'Soon shift 'em,' Watney said. 'Got their room number?'

'Desk clerk'll give it to you. Ask for the Jackson brothers.'

Billson and Watney went out and crossed the street to the hotel. At the desk, they were advised to go to Room 6.

Billson approached the room, with Watney just a pace behind him. They both stood at opposite sides of the door. Watney drew his gun, hoping that he'd have some excuse to shoot. Billson left his gun holstered, and knocked on the door.

'Who is it?' came a voice from inside.

'Deputy sheriff, sir,' Billson said. 'I was hoping to have

a word with you.'

'Is there any problem?'

'No, sir. We don't get many strangers in town and it makes the sheriff more at ease if we interview them. Nothing to worry about.'

'Just push the door open.'

Billson did so, and immediately a Colt .45 thrust against his cheek, hammer cocked, a finger resting tensely on the trigger.

Billson now saw another man come up behind Watney and press a revolver to the back of the deputy's head.

'Don't try anything, Deputy,' the man behind Watney said. 'Your brain will be full of lead in an instant, and you won't like it at all.'

Watney swore softly. He loosened his grip from his gun, and pointed it into the air. The man behind relieved him of it, and said, 'Why don't you two *gentlemen* step inside the room and we can discuss this?'

Billson nodded. 'We don't want any trouble. . . .'

'You should have thought of that before you came looking for it.' The man in the doorway gestured for Billson and Watney to enter.

'Allow me to introduce myself,' the man said as he continued pacing backwards. 'I'm James Jackson, and this is my brother Finn. Just move slowly, and there'll be no accidents.'

Billson walked forward, his hands in the air. As he entered the room, Finn came up behind Billson and took his gun from him.

James Jackson pointed his gun at Billson, and the other man continued to aim at Watney.

Nodding towards Watney, James said, 'Finn, why don't

you frisk this gentleman?'

Finn patted down Watney, and found a smaller gun concealed in his right boot.

'Tricky,' James said. 'Tie him to a chair.'

Finn took a rope, expertly tied Watney's hands behind his back, sat him down, and tied the two loose ends tightly to the chair-back. Then he bound Watney's legs together.

James took aim at Billson, and Finn frisked him, finding nothing.

'Do take a seat,' James said to Billson.

'Aren't you going to tie me up?'

'That wouldn't be very neighbourly of me, would it? Now to the point. We hadn't broken any laws.'

Billson said, 'True. But the sheriff don't like strangers in town. We've come to decide whether or not you should be allowed to remain here.'

Jackson said, 'I think that remaining here is something for me and my brother to decide.'

Something nagged at Billson. Something seemed familiar about these men.

Jackson continued. 'Why didn't the sheriff come himself?'

'He's a very busy man.'

'Too busy to make a neighbourly call on some visitors to this fine town. That's not very nice.'

'I'll kill yuh for this,' Watney raged through gritted teeth.

'Not if I kill you first,' Jackson said. Then he turned to Billson. 'I really don't like your colleague.'

Billson said, 'I don't care for him that much myself.'

Jackson said, 'I don't think this town is particularly hospitable. I think that we might be moving on sooner than we expected.'

'I think that might be for the best,' Billson said.

Watney growled, and struggled with his bonds.

Jackson stuck his gun against Watney's face. 'You can just stop struggling. You're making me nervous.'

Watney snarled, 'I'll kill yuh. I'll kill yuh both.'

'Shut up,' Jackson said. 'You're beginning to annoy me.'

Billson realized why the face was so familiar. James Jackson, indeed. Fairly obvious alias. This was Jesse James. He'd seen their faces on Wanted posters. Abernathy had fictionalized their exploits in the book that Emmy had read to Bain. Some coincidence. He'd heard there were two strangers in the saloon, talking to Abernathy. He wondered if it was not an accident that they had come here. Abernathy knew them, maybe, and was plotting something. Could it be that the dime novelist knew the truth?

The James brothers and their gang, he knew, were a tough outfit. Swiggard was not like them, although he had imagined that he was, but he had always gone for easy targets.

Billson said, 'You know, Mr Jackson, tying up a law officer in pursuance of his duty is a criminal offence. We could lock you up for that.'

Jesse said, 'You're in no position to do that. In fact, I think we'll tie you up as well. Finn, tie this gentleman up.'

Billson submitted to being tied up. Struggling wouldn't do him any good. As Frank James secured him, Jesse James collected their belongings.

Jesse said, 'Well, deputies, it hasn't been a pleasure doing business with you. I'm sure that after we leave it won't be long before the chambermaid finds you.'

Jesse tipped his hat, and the two brothers left. Billson heard the key turn in the lock, no doubt a precaution in case they got free sooner than expected, and then heard footsteps receding down the corridor.

Jesse and Frank sneaked out of the hotel when the desk clerk's back was turned.

They had been undecided about whether to stay neutral after they'd heard Gunn and Abernathy tell the tale of Swiggard the night before. But now they had made their minds up.

Jesse said, 'Frank, why don't we just take a ride out to the Hardin ranch and volunteer our services to the Reverend Gunn.'

'Sounds like a good idea to me, brother of mine.'

CHAPTER TEN

Savage realized when he'd heard from Billson and Watney about what had happened in the hotel that Abernathy must be up to no good. He told them not to mention the matter to the sheriff – he wanted to do a bit of investigating first. So he made sure that the writer was in the saloon, while he was pretending to make the rounds of the town, and then set about going to his hotel room to see what he could find.

Having confirmed that Abernathy was in the saloon, he went into the hotel and scowled at the desk clerk.

'Mr Bain said I've got to get something that Mr Abernathy needs from his room. Gimme the key.'

The clerk sniffed at Savage, but took the key from its place on the rack and slid it across the counter at Savage. Savage scooped it up, then crossed the lobby to the stairs and rushed up them two at a time. As he went, he heard a faint tutting from the clerk. Savage scoffed. *Bain hired you, mister*, he thought, *he can just as easily fire you – all it needs is my say-so.*

Savage loped along the corridor to Abernathy's room, slipped the key into the lock, then went inside what the

writer thought of as his private domain. Savage would
soon see if Abernathy was keeping any secrets from them.
He surveyed the room. Very neat and tidy. Abernathy was
clearly a methodical man. No papers left lying around.
Savage looked in the closet. Clothes hung neatly.

Savage inspected the bureau by the window, which
Abernathy was using as his writing desk, evidenced by the
pen and ink and the tidy pile of blank paper. No trouble
to break open the bureau for a thief of Savage's calibre.
He had the top drawer open in an instant, manipulating
the lock with the blade of his pocket knife. A quick
rummage through the drawer showed that there was a
manuscript, which was exactly what Savage expected to
find. Abernathy had been hired to write a book, so that
was clearly what he was doing. Savage glanced at the top
page of the pile of quarto papers, and found that in block
capitals, it was titled 'NATHAN BAIN: AMERICAN
HERO'.

So Abernathy *was* writing the book that he was con-
tracted to write. Then why was he hanging about with
undesirables and strangers?

Ever suspicious, Savage swiftly prised open the next
drawer down. And found another manuscript, entitled
'SWIGGARD: AMERICAN VILLAIN'. *What the hell?* Savage
lifted it out of the drawer and placed it on the top of the
bureau. He flicked through the book, reading odd
snatches of it. Somehow, Abernathy knew all about
Swiggard, and what had happened to the real Nathan
Bain. How could Abernathy possibly have known this?
Savage saw to his disgust his own name in this account of
Swiggard's villainy. If this ever got out, they would be finished. Destroyed utterly. They would be taken into jail,

tried and most likely hanged for various crimes including several murders. As a precaution, in case Swiggard were to turn on him like he had with others including Cal, Savage had always made sure that Swiggard carried out at least one killing on most of their raids. Swiggard was unable to shoot worth a damn, but he couldn't miss when his gun barrel was pressed into the victim's forehead or chest.

This manuscript, which looked more or less finished, must be destroyed before it could fall into the hands of anybody else, and Abernathy would have to be disposed of.

Savage had to make a decision. Should he wait here for Abernathy to return, and then take him somewhere to kill him? Obviously, there would be questions to answer if he killed him here. Everybody in town knew that Abernathy didn't carry a gun, so it would be unbelievable that Savage could kill him in self-defence.

Swiggard would have to be told about this, so that they could act together, or perhaps along with Billson and Watney, to trick Abernathy to come with them. Once they had the writer in their grasp, it would be a simple matter to make him disappear, as they had done to several people over the years.

Swiggard was not going to like it, not one little bit. He had been banking on the book making a reputation for him that would allow him to be free of this measly little town, and to be able to make a real fortune and achieve high political office. Savage had heard Swiggard compare himself to the former President, Ulysses S. Grant. He so believed his own lies about being a war hero that he thought that he could become governor of this territory, maybe even aspire to the highest office in the land.

Savage always laughed at the thought of that. How could that happen? A braggart and a coward like Swiggard, becoming President? Not to mention that he was a thief and a murderer.

Savage had a thought. He looked again at the first manuscript he had found in the bureau. It looked more or less complete. There were very few crossings-out, and Abernathy's neat hand was easily legible. This could still be the book that Swiggard had hoped for. In fact, with Abernathy out of the way, Swiggard could pass himself off as the real author of the book. It was narrated in the first person, as by Nathan Bain. When Abernathy *disappeared*, they would be able to present the work as Bain's own writing. Savage wasn't much of a reader, so he couldn't tell whether the writing was any good, but it would certainly satisfy Swiggard.

Savage decided that the best thing he could do would be to lock the 'good' manuscript back in the desk, and to take the 'bad' one away with him. That would be the evidence he would show to Swiggard to prove that Abernathy was double-crossing him. Then they could get rid of Abernathy, maybe push him down into Calvert Canyon, where he'd likely never be found. Several of their enemies had disappeared there over the years. Then they could recover the manuscript at their convenience, and Swiggard could arrange to have it published as his own work.

Savage reckoned that was a good plan. He chuckled at the thought that he was the real brains of this outfit, that Swiggard would be nobody without him and would have ended up dead at the end of a rope or shot in the back years ago if it hadn't been for him.

The only thing that bothered Savage was how Abernathy had found out the truth about Swiggard. Nobody in the town knew about him, and they all believed that he was Nathan Bain. The only people who knew Swiggard's identity were his deputies. Two of the men who used to ride with them, Howard and Cornell, had died in a shooting that had gone wrong. And Cal Cannon had argued once too often with the boss, who had asked Savage to rid him of the troublesome black. Savage had shot Cannon, and thrown him down a ravine, so the only people remaining who knew the truth were Swiggard himself, Savage, and Billson and Watney. But that had to mean that one of the other deputies was a traitor. It was quite impossible that Swiggard had ever let anything slip to Emmy about his past. Even if he had, he wouldn't have gone into the detail that Abernathy so obviously knew about. No, it had to be Billson or Watney. Savage would have to keep an eye on them.

Savage took up the 'bad' manuscript, and made his way out of the room, locking it behind him. He then swiftly left the hotel.

He didn't look back as he crossed the lobby. Had he done so, he would have noticed that he was being watched.

'I'll kill him. I'll tear him apart with muh bare hands.'

Swiggard was taking it as calmly as Savage had expected. A purple-faced rage. If Savage had been standing any closer, he would have received a pounding from Swiggard's fists. As it was, the sheriff's desk was jumping up and down from the hammering that Swiggard's pudgy fists were giving it.

'Calm down, Mark.'

Using Swiggard's real name got a reaction. 'I've told you over and over again. Don't use that name. My name is Nathan Bain.'

'OK, Nathan. Now we know that Abernathy knows the truth. . . .'

'Lies!' Swiggard insisted. 'Poisonous, foul lies! I don't know where he got this . . . this . . . filth from, but we need to put a stop to it right now. Do yuh happen to know where this treacherous bastard is right now?'

'Uh . . . I think he's in the saloon.'

'Yuh think? *Yuh think?* I don't pay yuh to think. I pay yuh to do mah bidding, and tuh shoot people.'

'I'm certain Abernathy is in the saloon.'

'Good man. I like the cut of your jib. Remind me to give you a raise.'

Savage thought that he would remind himself to not remind Swiggard. A punch in the eye was what he usually got when the subject of a wage increase was discussed.

'Can yuh be trusted to get Abernathy over here without him suspecting something's up?'

'Sure thing, boss.'

'Well, go get him. And see if yuh can round up Billson and Watney while yuh're about it.'

Savage nodded.

'Well, why are yuh still here?'

Savage left the office and ran across to the saloon to find Abernathy.

Abernathy was no longer in the saloon. He and Gunn had sneaked out the back way when Geoffrey had told them that Savage was coming to get Abernathy with the intention of arranging his murder.

'I'd really like to outlive the sheriff and the deputies,' Abernathy said when Geoffrey told him that.

'Me too,' Gunn agreed. 'Shall we beat a retreat?'

'Seems like a good idea to me. Geoffrey, I notice you came in the back way. That's where we'll leave.'

They got out the door, just as the batwings were swinging open and Savage and the other two deputies were coming through the doorway.

'We'll have to get a move on. They'll realize very soon that we've slipped oot the back door. Lucky for you, Fred, that I borrowed Miss Emmy's buggy to come here tonight and that I parked it oot of sight of the sheriff, because it's his wife's carriage.'

'Lead the way, Guthrie,' Abernathy said.

Gunn led them down the alleyway to Second Street, where the less rowdy businesses were set up, so that they wouldn't be troubled by the rough crowd who frequented the saloon, the whorehouse and the gambling tent. As they made their way there, Abernathy questioned Geoffrey about why the deputies were after him.

'Sheriff wants you killed.'

'And me such an agreeable fellow, too. Do you know why he wants me killed?'

'Yes, sir,' Geoffrey said.

'Well then, tell me why he wants me killed.'

'Because you've written the truth about him, about him being a deserter from the army, and a criminal, and a murderer. And an . . . imposer?'

'Impostor. The man you know as Nathan Bain is really a lying, murderous thug named Mark Swiggard.'

Geoffrey shook his head. 'Never liked him.'

'Me neither,' the writer concurred. 'After about the first

two seconds in his company. So why did you follow Savage?'

'Well, sir. He told the desk clerk that Mr Bain had asked him to bring something of yours from your room. I knew that you had gone to the saloon, so I didn't believe him. I saw him coming down the stairs carrying some of your papers. I remember you telling me that you never let anybody see any of your work until it's finished, and I didn't think it was finished. So I sneaked out of the hotel and followed him.'

'*Geoffrey*, really? You deserted your post?'

'Yes, sir, I did.'

'Good lad. Well done.'

'So I followed him across the street, sneaked round the side of the jailhouse and overheard him tell the sheriff that you were writing two books, one of them about the sheriff being a criminal. And I heard them discuss that they wanted to kill you.'

'And you decided to warn me?'

'I did, sir. I like you. You're one of the few people I've ever met who's treated me decent.'

'Geoffrey, I'm touched. Will you be in trouble for deserting your post?'

'I think so, sir. They'll probably realize who it was who warned you they were coming.'

'Gunn, I think that we'd better invite this young man to join our band of conspirators. What do you say?'

'The more the merrier,' the Scotsman said.

They had now reached Emmy's buggy, and Gunn quickly took the hobbles off the horses. 'There's room up here for all three of us. How would you like a life of adventure, young sir?'

105

'It has to be better than toting bags and dodging out of the way of slaps from the desk clerk.' He jumped up onto the buggy's driving seat and slipped over to the other end, leaving room for Abernathy and Gunn to climb up beside him, which they did.

Gunn said, 'Well, Hardin's hayloft is becoming quite the hideout. Ah well, there's definitely room for two more.'

Then Gunn set the horses to drive back to the Hardin ranch.

CHAPTER ELEVEN

Brendan and Joseph were working in the corral, breaking in the colts.

The corral was set some hundred yards from the main Hardin house, and could be observed through the windows or from the veranda, where Emmy Hardin was sitting out on this unusually warm October day, reading a book, glancing occasionally at the young men working the colts, and watching her daughter.

Clemmy was playing near the corral. Her mother had warned her not to get too close. She was big enough now to climb up onto the fence posts, and Emmy was concerned that she might fall. She saw that Brendan was glancing over at the girl, then he left the saddling and went over to the fence to speak to Clemmy. Emmy saw him smile and speak to the girl. She smiled back at him, and spoke to him. Then she jumped off the fence, and wandered away. The boy watched the girl for a few moments, then turned and went back to the horses.

Emmy sipped a lemonade, and picked up her book. It was *Vengeance in Virginia* by Flint Andrews, one of the dime novels she had borrowed from the literate ranch hand.

107

She had caught the occasional glimpse of Mr Abernathy, and he looked like an eastern gentleman, or at least what she imagined such a man would be. The book was silly, and the author didn't even seem to know the difference between a sheriff and a marshal, but she liked it anyway.

Then she heard a splash.

She looked up, and couldn't see Clemmy.

'Clemmy!' She began to run down towards the stream. Clemmy had been told many times not to play beside the water.

She saw Brendan vault over the fence, with the Indian boy following hard at his heels.

Emmy was still about twenty yards from the stream when she saw Brendan dive into the water. Although they called it a stream, it was wide enough to be considered a river, and was deep enough that a child could drown in it.

Time seemed to slow for Emmy. It felt that Brendan must have been under the water for minutes.

As she reached the bank, Brendan broke the surface. Emmy cried out when she didn't see Clemmy, but then Brendan's other arm surfaced, and the girl was cradled in it. Joseph reached the bank, stepped into the water and pulled Brendan towards the bank. He then took hold of Clemmy and laid her on the ground.

The child looked dead. Emmy screamed again. Brendan, dripping wet, knelt over the girl. Joseph leaned over, and whispered in Brendan's ear. Brendan looked up at him, nodded, then moved behind the girl's head. Taking hold of her wrists, he pulled her arms towards him, not hurrying, then brought them back below her chin, pressing them hard down onto her chest. Then he repeated the process, each iteration of the movement lasting about five seconds. On the seventh press of the girl's chest, she spluttered, then gasped, and started to cough up water. She looked around, saw the two boys kneeling over her, and then saw her mother. She began to whimper.

'Mommy, I falled in the water.'

Emmy snatched her up and hugged her tightly. Then she looked at Brendan, and smiled.

'I know you did, darling,' Emmy said to the girl. 'This nice man dived in after you and saved you.'

The little girl looked up and said, 'Thank oo, mister.'

Brendan said, 'You're very welcome, Miss Clemmy. You can call me Brenbren.'

Emmy gave Brendan a quizzical look.

He said, 'She reminds me of my sister. She used to call me Brenbren.'

Emmy beamed at him. 'Whatever your name is, you've performed a miracle.'

'No, ma'am. Not a miracle. It was Joseph's idea.'

'Some kind of special Indian medicine?' she said.

'No, ma'am,' Joseph said. 'I read about it in a book. *The Silvester Method*, it's called. I told Brendan about it at the time, and we practised it. It was a sort of game.'

'That's right, ma'am,' Brendan said. 'Never thought we'd ever have to do it for real.'

Still clutching her daughter, Emmy moved closer to Brendan, and kissed him on the cheek. Brendan blushed.

'I thank you for saving my daughter. I'll tell my father, and he'll reward you.'

'That's really not necessary,' Brendan said.

'Speak for yourself,' Joseph said.

Emmy looked at the two young men. 'But what are we

doing standing out here like this? You're both soaking wet. And so is Clemmy. You'd better get indoors, or you could get pleurisy.'

'Just what I was thinking, ma'am,' Brendan said. 'We've got dry clothes in the barn.'

'Well, I'll see you later, Mr Brenbren Brennan.'

'Glad to be of service, Miss Emmy,' Brendan said.

Emmy turned and took her daughter back into the main house. As she reached the veranda she turned and looked again at Brendan and Joseph, who were making their way into the barn.

Brendan and Joseph changed out of their wet clothes and put on dry clothing.

Hardin himself came into the barn, and approached them.

'Are you looking for Mr Gunn?' Brendan said.

'No, *Mister* Brennan.' *Mister*, not Brendan. Brendan wondered what kind of trouble he was in.

Hardin must have seen it in his face. 'Brendan, nothing to worry about. My daughter has told me what happened. She's very pleased with you. She's very pleased with you both. I'm pleased with you too. You saved my granddaughter.'

'We only did what had to be done,' Brendan said.

'But if it hadn't been you two, if it had been one of the ranch hands. . . .' Hardin seemed lost for words. Then he spoke again. 'It was you, and you knew how to save Clemmy from drowning. You . . . revived her.'

'It was nothing, sir.'

'I won't be contradicted on that matter, boy.'

Brendan bowed his head.

'My daughter insists that the two of you join us in the big house for dinner this evening.'

Joseph looked surprised. 'Both of us?'

Hardin nodded. 'Both of you. From what I hear, it was you who knew what to do to save the girl.'

'But it was Brendan who did it, sir? He's the one who deserves the credit, and any kind of reward should go to him.'

'My daughter insists. And I do too.'

Joseph looked doubtful, and shook his head.

'Something the matter, lad?'

'No, sir.' Joseph hesitated, but Hardin waited for him to give a proper answer. 'It's just that . . . well. . . .'

'Spit it out.'

'Well . . . I've never been invited to dinner before.'

Hardin laughed, and so did Brendan.

Then Brendan thought for a moment, and said, 'I've never been invited to dinner either.'

Hardin snorted, trying to prevent his laughter from turning into guffaws. 'Never mind that. I'll expect you over at the house about seven.'

Then Hardin turned and left the barn.

Later, back in the barn, Joseph said, 'You should have seen Brendan's face, Guthrie. He didn't know what to do, or how to hold the soup spoon, or the fish knife.'

'My nephew, the savage,' Gunn said.

Brendan blushed. 'Well, I'd never been to a dinner like that. Family dinners at home were nothing like that, and eating customs on the reservation are totally different. But Joseph did just fine.'

'I remembered what to do from a book on etiquette.'

Brendan scoffed. 'Some Lakota brave you are, nose always stuck in a book.'

'The only good thing about *wasicun* culture is books.'

'Now, laddies. No need to argue.'

Joseph laughed again. 'And he didn't know where to look when Miss Emmy was fawning all over him.'

'She was *not*!' Brendan said.

'Was too. With her parents right there. And not just because you saved her daughter from drowning. I think she likes you.'

'I don't think so. Anyway, she's married to that monster.'

Gunn said, 'I think she regrets that.'

Brendan said, 'I can't understand why she married that creep.'

Joseph said, 'You like her too, don't you? As much as she likes you?'

Brendan blushed.

'You do, don't you?'

'Leave the laddie alone, Joseph,' Gunn said. 'It's perfectly obvious that he has a liking for the young lady.'

Brendan said, 'What if I have? She's still married.'

Joseph looked thoughtful. 'In the tribe, if a woman doesn't like her husband, she tells him to get lost. If he won't, then the chief will banish him. Then she takes up with another husband who'll treat her better.'

'Very sensible,' Gunn said.

CHAPTER TWELVE

Brendan began spending more time playing with the child than working on the ranch, or so it seemed to Hardin.

Brendan liked her, but he found himself liking the mother even more. And he got the impression Hardin was encouraging the attention he was paying to his daughter. Or was it the attention she was paying to him? But he had spent so long away from the world of the *wasicun* that he was unsure – could he be misunderstanding the situation?

He was not inexperienced in the ways of women, but the women he knew were Lakota. He had almost entered into a marriage with Eagle Feather, an attractive girl of about his own age, until he had found out that she only wanted to get closer to Red Ghost, who showed no interest in her.

The ways of white women were a mystery to him. He was baffled. He wanted to ask his uncle for advice, but Gunn seemed reluctant to discuss the fairer sex. Joseph was little better as a confidant, because although he knew something of love between white men and women, it all came from novels.

He'd asked Mr Abernathy, who'd said, 'Kiss the girl,

dammit. Everybody can see that she likes you.'

'But maybe she's only being polite, because I rescued her daughter from drowning.'

'You are a fool, boy. That may have been why she noticed you in the first place, but it's obvious she likes you.'

'You really think so?' Brendan was shaking his head, not quite ready to believe what the writer was telling him. But he was smiling, too.

The meeting hadn't exactly been called or planned, it just sort of emerged once the James brothers had allied with Gunn and the others. Abernathy reckoned they now had sufficient force to go up against Swiggard and his men, and Gunn agreed.

Hardin acted as the chairman. It took place in his dining room. Mrs Hardin had gone on a picnic with Emmy and Clemmy, having been asked to make themselves scarce that morning.

Gunn surveyed the men gathered around the dining table. Hardin, as was his custom, sat at the head of the table. Gunn was seated at the opposite end. Brendan, Joseph and Abernathy on one side, and Jesse and Frank James, and Cal on the other. Geoffrey the bellboy squeezed in beside Cal. He was part of the gang now.

A motley crew, Gunn thought.

Hardin said, 'I think, gentlemen, that it's time that we came up with a plan to get rid of Swiggard.'

Gunn nodded in agreement. 'That's what we need tae do, all right. But how dae we go about it? If it were up tae me, I'd just sneak intae his house and blow his brains out.'

Jesse said, 'Now, Guthrie. What happened to "Thou

114

shalt not kill"?'

'I'd make an exception in his case. But you're right, Joshua. God, or Wakan Tanka, told me it's all right to kill that odious Swiggard. But while supernatural forces have given me permission to kill him, the law hasn't. This territory might be a bit wild, but it's not completely lawless. If I shot him at point blank range, or in the back, I'd have a murder charge to answer for. And while I'd happily die to see the world rid o' him, I'd rather live to see a world that didn't have him in it.'

Joseph said, 'I agree. We have to get him to draw first, so that it's self-defence when we shoot him.'

Cal said, 'I've never seen him draw his gun to shoot with it. He kills, I've seen him do that. But he puts the gun barrel right to the head or the chest of unarmed or sleeping people so that he can't miss. You'll never get him to draw in a fair fight. He boasts that he's won hundreds of gunfights, but it's a lie.'

Gunn said, 'We need some way to get him away from his deputies. We outnumber them, but *they* are ruthless killers. And at least two of us can't shoot.'

'It's a problem,' Hardin agreed. 'Anybody got any ideas.'

Everybody in the room was silent.

Eventually, Jesse said, 'It's not so easy to get rid of the bad guy when he's the legal authority, is it?'

Abernathy stroked his chin. 'I wonder. . . .'

'You got an idea, Fred?' Gunn asked.

'Maybe.' Abernathy paused, shaking his head and hesitating. 'It's . . . it's kind of vague. Something I remember from somewhere, but its context isn't clear to me. My trick memory lets me remember everything, but not always where it came from.'

The men waited expectantly, and after a time Abernathy's eyebrows raised, and he smiled.

Hardin said, 'You got an idea, Fred?'

Yes.' Abernathy said. 'We rob the bank.'

They all tried to speak at once.

It wasn't a formal meeting, so the chairman didn't have a gavel. Hardin unholstered his gun, gripped it by the barrel, and rapped the table with the butt. Not too hard – Mrs Hardin would have had a fit if she saw any damage.

The men quietened down, and Hardin said, 'What do you mean, Fred?'

'I remember reading about a bank robbery, I think it was in a dime novel. But it might have been a true story in a newspaper. A corrupt sheriff was operating his town as a personal fiefdom, much like Swiggard is doing in Misery. The town mayor nominally owned the bank, but the sheriff owned the mayor. He captured a gang of outlaws, and instead of bringing them to trial, he had them rob the bank for him. The deal was that the insurance company would recompense the bank for the loss of the money, and the outlaws would give the money back to the sheriff, which he would keep for himself. The outlaws would get to keep five per cent of the loot, and have their freedom.'

'Sounds good,' Gunn said. 'How did that story end?'

'One of the villain's deputies is more honest than him, and arranges for him to have an accident on the way to collecting the loot.'

'What kind of accident?' Jesse asked.

'His brain accidentally got in the way of a bullet.'

'That's the kind of accident that I favour,' Frank said.

'Provided it's happening to somebody I don't like.'

'I thought,' Abernathy said, 'that we could do something similar. We don't have a good deputy to arrange for a misfortune to befall Swiggard, but I'm sure we'll come up with something.'

'Sounds good to me,' Frank said.

Jesse nodded. 'And me. Robbery is our area of expertise, you might say.'

Hardin chuckled. 'I don't put money in that bank, because it's Bain's . . . Swiggard's . . . bank. The thought of him looking after my money fills me with revulsion. I bank at Medicine Falls, even though it's sixty miles away.'

'Of course, we wouldn't really be stealing the money,' Abernathy said.

'Pity,' Frank said.

'That wouldn't achieve what we want to do.'

Gunn agreed. 'We're not doing this for money. We're doing this to destroy that man.'

'Reverend, I'm shocked,' Abernathy said, but with a twinkle in his eye.

Gunn shrugged. 'I may be a man of the cloth, but I am a man. I won't stand idly by when there's a monster terrorizing decent people.'

Abernathy said, 'The idea of enriching himself by criminality is bound to appeal to his greed. Cal has told us that he hates doing anything that involves putting himself at risk. He doesn't have the guts to rob a bank or hold up a stagecoach, for instance. So we make him an offer. He knows, I'm certain, that Jesse and Frank are the two men who humiliated his deputies. I happen to know, because he told me, that he is in total awe of you two. That's why he hired me to write his autobiography, because he was so

117

impressed by the way I portrayed you in *Missouri Vengeance*. If you put the idea to him, Jesse, he'll listen to it. He'll be passing the idea off as his own once he takes a liking to it.'

Cal agreed. 'That's the way his mind works. I think he's incapable of thinking anything out for himself. Any plans or schemes he comes up with he gets them from Savage. He used to get some of them . . . in fact most of them . . . from me, I'm ashamed to admit, before I turned against him. Give him a notion that he likes, and he'll steal it from you. He'll claim that only a great genius like him can come up with such brilliant ideas.'

Abernathy turned towards Cal and said, 'Do you know whether or not the bank is insured or not?'

Cal shook his head. 'It used to be, when I was privy to these matters. I don't know about now.'

Geoffrey said, 'It's insured. I know it is.'

Gunn frowned. 'How do you know?'

'Nothing ever gets past a bellboy. We know everything that goes on in the hotel *and* the neighbourhood.'

Abernathy said, 'Then I think that a bit of outlawry on our part would answer very nicely.'

'I like it,' Hardin said. 'Are we all agreed that this is what we should do?'

Everybody around the table nodded.

'Well then, it's just a matter of working out the details of the plan. . . .'

CHAPTER THIRTEEN

Jesse James pushed open the door of the sheriff's office, and walked boldly in, stopping in front of the sheriff seated at his desk.

Swiggard looked up, blinking as the sunlight coming through the doorway dazzled him slightly. He squinted, and said, 'That you, Savage?'

'I've been called a savage in my day, but they mainly know me as Jesse James.'

'What yuh want?' Swiggard asked.

'You Nathan Bain?' Jesse asked.

'Yeah. Who wants to know?'

'I told you. I'm Jesse James.'

'Right. And I'm Ulysses S. Grant.'

Jesse James chuckled. 'I don't think so. I've seen a photograph of President Grant, and you look nothing like him. I heard tell that you go by the name of Nathan Bain.'

'What d'yuh mean by that?' the sheriff said.

'Only that I'm looking to give myself up to the sheriff here.'

'Why?'

'Myself and my brother, we had a run in with two of

your deputies. We tied them up.'

'Oh yeah,' Swiggard said. 'What yuh do that for?'

'They pointed a gun at us. I think that they wanted us to leave town.'

'We thought yuh was federal marshals. We've had trouble with federal lawmen in the past, and Pinkertons. They're all crooks, every last goddamn one of them. Seems I fit the description of some outlaw.'

'I wonder why that is?'

'What yuh suggesting?'

'Oh, nothing. It's just that it doesn't reflect well on me that you thought I looked like a lawman. I'm an outlaw, and a dangerous one. Price on my head and all that.'

'So what yuh want with me?'

'To give myself up to the great lawman Nathan Bain.'

Swiggard raised his eyebrows. 'It's good yuh realize who yuh dealing with here. I truly am a great law enforcer. The greatest. But I ain't so good that the outlaws give themselves up of their own voluntary. Usually have tuh shoot them. What's your angle? You're not really Jesse James.'

'Sure I am. Take a look at that Wanted poster over on the wall there. See that picture. That's me.'

Swiggard got up gingerly from his chair, walked over to the wall with the Wanted posters, and looked at it. Then he looked over at Jesse. 'Sure looks like you.'

'That's because it is me.'

'Well then, I guess you're under arrest.'

'Fine by me. Lead me to your best cell.'

'Cells are all the same.'

'The nearest one, then. Lead on, Macduff.'

'Who? My name's Bain. Who told yuh it wasn't? Bain, not Mack Duff.'

Jesse said, 'Never mind.' Then he walked towards the cell, stepped into it and pulled the door shut.

Swiggard didn't move.

Jesse said, 'What're you waiting for, Sheriff? Aren't you going to lock me in?'

Swiggard shook his head as if recovering from a daze. He reached over to the rack where the keys were kept and locked the cell door.

Jesse said, 'Well done, Mr Bain. You've managed to do what hundreds of lawmen have tried to do, but couldn't. You've captured Jesse James.'

'That's right.' Swiggard's face lit up, as if he realized what he had just done, and he smiled broadly. 'That's *right*! I caught yuh because I'm the greatest lawman in the west – hell, the whole country. I'll be a shoo-in fur Governor at the next election once I write about this in my book.'

Jesse chuckled, and shook his head. 'Governor? Bain, I'm surprised at you. You just want to be Governor, when the big prize is within your grasp.'

Swiggard frowned, and gave Jesse a hard stare. 'What yuh mean? What big prize?'

'I'm truly surprised that a great man of your calibre hasn't worked out that you're destined for the Presidency.'

Jesse could see Swiggard's face flushing in response to that. Fred had been right – that was the way to get the man interested.

'What'd yuh mean, *predisency*?'

Jesse patted the bars of the cell. 'Just that you don't want to be satisfied with being the law in this pipsqueak town. You're too good for that. And why settle for just being the Governor in this forsaken territory? You would look just fine and dandy lording it over the whole union in the White House. You could be President of the United States.'

Jesse knew that this was Swiggard's ambition because Fred had told him. Swiggard was rapt now, entranced by what Jesse had to say.

'You could write a book about your greatness as a war hero and a lawman, and how you captured the great Jesse James.'

The sheriff was nodding in agreement.

'But even with a book telling the world how great you are, that won't be enough to get you to the top.'

'Why not?' Swiggard said.

'Because you need money. Lots and lots of money.'

'I got money.'

'Not enough,' Jesse said. 'You'll need far more money than that. You'll need to get vast quantities, and invest it in companies that'll get you even more. You'd never raise enough just from the taxation in this town.'

'I got plenty.'

'Not enough, though. But think what you could do if every cent deposited in the bank was yours?'

Swiggard scratched his forehead. The idea was beginning to penetrate his thick skull.

Jesse said, 'What you need, is to rob the bank.'

'Huh?'

'Think about it, Bain. If the whole lot was yours, you could use it to get yourself a real fortune, enough to mount a political campaign like no other in history. You'd be sure to win.'

Swiggard pushed his hat brim upwards, and rubbed his chin, clearly intrigued.

'I'm no bank robber. And why would I rob mah own bank?'

Jesse noted that Swiggard wasn't even bothering to conceal that he was the bank's owner.

Jesse told the sheriff, 'Because you'll have the money insured. And you don't need to worry about robbing the bank. You're looking at one of the greatest bank robbers there's ever been.'

Swiggard frowned, then remembered who this man was. 'That's right. You're Jesse James. . . .'

'Yes. And my brother is nearly as good a bank robber as I am. We're able to call on a few associates, and we'll do the robbing for you.'

Swiggard thought about this, then frowned. 'But how does I know you won't run away with the money?'

'Mr Bain, I'm surprised at you. I'm a man of my word. We're going to make sure that you get what's coming to you.'

Swiggard pursed his lips, and nodded, slowly coming to a decision. Then he said, 'I've got a great idea. I'll let yuh go if yuh rob the bank for me.'

Jesse chuckled. 'Only a great genius could think of that. I'm impressed, Mr Bain. You're clearly a great criminal mastermind, and you're wasted working in law enforcement. What's in it for me, though?'

'Mighty good of yuh to *reckernize* greatness when yuh see it. As for you, well in *addiction* to mah *magnaminity* in letting yuh go, yuh can keep five . . . no, two . . . per cent of the booty.'

Jesse reached through the cell door, turned the key, which was still in the lock, pulled the door open, and came forward to shake the sheriff's pudgy hand. 'Mr Bain, very generous of you. Two per cent. You've got a deal.'

Jesse shook Swiggard's hand, holding on to it far longer than normal, a trick that had been suggested by Cal. He could tell that because the fat man wasn't trying to let go, he was well and truly hooked.

CHAPTER
FOURTEEN

It was time to put the plan into action.

Jesse and Frank knew that they needed more than just the two of them, so they recruited Gunn, Abernathy and Geoffrey. Abernathy wouldn't be much use if there were to be any shooting, but his physical presence should be enough. Gunn could shoot, Jesse knew, because they'd had a target practice contest the previous day, and the Scot had run him close, and had easily come second ahead of Frank. And Geoffrey, it turned out, was nearly as good a shot as Frank.

Brendan and Joseph had gone ahead, taking up look-out positions across the street from the bank. They knew how to shoot, but were more comfortable with bows and arrows. Jesse hoped that they wouldn't be needed.

'OK, boys,' Jesse said, as they approached the rise above the town. 'Get ready.'

They pulled up their bandannas so that they covered their faces. Jesse nodded to Hardin, who had been following behind with a wagon, to wait there with it in case it was needed. Bank robbery was always risky, even when the owner wanted it robbed.

They spurred their mounts. Abernathy's improving horsemanship allowed him to keep up. He still didn't look comfortable on horseback, but it had been a couple of days since he had last fallen off.

Teaching him to use a gun had been another matter.

They soon arrived at the bank. Jesse was first to make his way through the entrance. Having cased the place three days earlier, he knew exactly what to do. There was a guard just to the side of the door, and Jesse punched him in the face before he could react. A woman customer saw him fall to the ground, and opened her mouth to scream. Frank was instantly upon her, covered her mouth, and said, 'Shut up, lady.'

She bit him. He winced and pulled his hand free from her mouth. Frank made a fist with his bleeding hand and socked her in the jaw. She was too shocked to cry out.

'Begging your pardon, ma'am,' Frank said. 'I know it's wrong to disrespect a lady, but you shouldn't go biting a fella.'

Jesse jumped over the counter, grabbed one of the two tellers and put a gun to the man's temple, shielding himself from the other teller with the first man's body. He saw that they both had handguns. Time was, bank tellers wouldn't have been armed. Was there no trust these days? He relieved his 'hostage' of his firearm, and instructed the other teller to place his gun carefully, and slowly, onto the counter. Once it was there, Frank slipped it into his pocket.

The three inexperienced bandits took up their agreed positions, Gunn guarding the doorway, Abernathy pretending to look menacing, while Geoffrey – for all his youth – managed to look like a seasoned desperado, with two guns trained on the customers he had pushed to the floor. As agreed beforehand, Gunn, Geoffrey and the writer did not speak, although the former bellboy managed the occasional fierce growl to impress on his captives that he meant business.

Frank handed a sack to one of the tellers. Jesse said, 'Just put the money from the drawers into this sack. Quick as you can.'

The teller frowned, but pulled out the drawers and tipped their contents into the sack.

Frank turned his attention to the other teller. He handed him another sack and pressed his revolver into his ribs, pushing him towards the safe.

Jesse said, 'Now, sir. Please put all the money from the safe into that sack. Just the money. We're not interested in anything else that might be there.'

The teller shrugged, swung the safe door open sufficiently to reach in and quickly pushed the cash into the sack.

Frank took the sack, tied it closed, and threw it and himself over the counter. He collected the other sack as he went, all the while keeping his gun aimed at the teller.

Jesse said, 'Good doing business with you. One last thing, don't anybody try to raise the alarm or even leave the premises for at least ten minutes. We've got somebody out there with a shotgun aimed right at the bank entrance. Any of you comes out that door, you'll be filled with lead. I wouldn't recommend that.'

Jesse nodded to the gang. Gunn exited first, followed by Geoffrey and Abernathy. Before Frank left he fired his gun at the tellers. The two men winced, but there was no sound from the gun other than two clicks. Jesse shook his head. Abernathy had been equipped with an empty gun, just in case there was an accident in the heat of the moment, but Frank must have unloaded his before they set off. Jesse would find time later to lambaste him for taking such a crazy chance.

Frank slipped out of the bank, laughing as he went.

Jesse said, 'Although my colleague's gun wasn't loaded, mine definitely is. And I assure you that the man watching the bank will shoot you if you show your faces before . . . let's see now . . . nineteen minutes past two by the clock on the wall.'

He pulled the bank door open, and glanced out. The rest of the gang had mounted up and were waiting for him. Frank had untethered Jesse's horse, and they were ready to go.

Jesse went through the door, ran to his mount, leapt into the saddle, and the motley gang of bank robbers turned to head out of town, back to the wagon where Hardin was waiting.

Hardin and Cal were there at the rendezvous.

'How did it go?' Hardin said, as the James brothers halted by the wagon.

'Easy,' Jesse said. 'Like finding money in the street.'

'I wanna do that again,' Geoffrey said, jumping down from his horse. 'That was fun.'

Gunn rode up, chuckling. 'I really shouldn't have liked that as much as I did. Now I can see why people turn to sin so readily.'

Abernathy arrived and eased himself off his horse. As he got to the ground, he tugged at his pants leg, and moved a little gingerly.

'That was fantastic,' Abernathy said. 'When can we do it again?'

'Calm down, Fred,' Jesse said. 'That was a one-time deal for you.'

'Come on, Jesse. If the writing doesn't work out, I want to take up robbing banks. Is it always as exciting as this?'

'It's a dangerous game, Fred,' Frank said. 'But it's the only way we can make a living since the Yankees ruined this country.'

Jesse said, 'It *is* exciting though. But stick to what you're good at, Fred. You can't shoot, and you can barely ride. You wouldn't last five minutes as an outlaw.'

'Well, I'm going to use this experience in a book.'

'I'll look forward to reading it,' Frank said.

Jesse said to Hardin, 'We won't be needing your wagon after all. Nothing went wrong.'

'Then I'll head back to the ranch.'

Just as Hardin was about drive off, two riders appeared on the horizon, galloping fast. Jesse and Frank drew their guns, but holstered them again when they recognized Brendan and Joseph.

'How did it go?' Jesse asked.

'Just as expected,' Joseph said. 'The tellers came out after ten minutes, and ran to the sheriff. He didn't come and look at the bank, but he had Savage and the two other deputies round up some men for a posse. Then Savage led the posse eastwards.'

Gunn said, 'The opposite direction from us.'

'Exactly. Swiggard wanted to make sure that the posse wouldn't catch us.'

Cal said, 'Swiggard won't have told them what the plan

is. He doesn't trust them the way he used to trust me.'

Jesse said, 'Then it's time to put the next part of the plan into operation. Fred?'

Abernathy nodded, and opened up his saddle-bag. He took out a couple of sheets of paper and handed them to Joseph.

Jesse said to Joseph, 'You head back into town and set the trap for Swiggard. You can meet us once that's done.'

Joseph carefully slid the paper into his quiver, remounted and rode back towards Misery.

Then Hardin set off to his ranch, and the rest of the gang headed to the location for their showdown with Swiggard.

CHAPTER FIFTEEN

Bain sat anxiously in his office, surprised that he hadn't heard something by now. He began to feel a queasy sensation in his stomach. *Must just be indigestion,* he thought. He never got nervous, not ever. That was one thing that he prided himself on. The fearless Nathan Bain. That would have made a good title for the book that Abernathy was helping him with. *Had* been helping. . . .

He wished that Cal was still with him; he had been so dependable. He didn't trust Savage. The man was useful with a gun, and handy with his fists, but there was something shifty about him, as if he resented his boss's superior abilities as a lawman.

There was a sudden whoosh above his head, then a sharp thud on the wall behind him. He turned and saw that it was an arrow.

An arrow? Indians? He couldn't believe it. He hadn't encountered any Indians for years. They knew better than to come near this town. He ducked down, not because he was afraid, oh no, but so as to manoeuvre to the window to see what was going on. He crawled around his desk on all fours and made his way to the window.

131

Carefully, he raised his eyes above the window sill. Nobody there. Some cowardly Indian must have made this brazen attempt on his life then run off.

Then he turned and looked back at the arrow. He saw what he had failed to notice at first, a piece of paper skewered on it. His legendary powers of observation must have been affected by the dyspepsia in his stomach. He belched loudly, thinking that might clear his head.

He went to the piece of paper and saw that it had writing on it. He took it to his desk, laid it down and sat down to look at it. The writing must be some kind of illegible scrawl because he couldn't make it out. He reached into his desk and took out the eyeglasses that Emmeline had insisted that he buy. His vision was perfect, but he didn't know what was upsetting him today, and he thought that it wouldn't hurt to use some magnification, just this once.

He ran his finger along the words, which had somehow come into sharper focus, slowly mouthing the syllables as he did so. The note read: 'Swiggard, we're onto you.'

Swiggard? Who in hell is Swiggard? Bain had almost no awareness now that he had not always been Nathan Bain. He read on: 'If you want to find out what has happened to the money from the bank robbery, come to the disused swing station at Cripple Creek. Come alone.

'If you don't come, you'll never see your money again.'

It was signed: 'Flint Andrews'.

Who the hell is Flint Andrews? Then he remembered it was Abernathy's phony name. Was he some kind of criminal that he needed to use an alias? What a fool Cal had been to engage this criminal Abernathy! If Bain ever caught up with Cal, he'd make him pay, for sure. No, wait a minute.

Cal had already been disposed of. *Something I ate, sure enough*, he thought, *must be affecting my normally perfect memory*. Ah well, if these robbers got away, there was still the insurance. He could always exaggerate the amount of money that had been stolen. No need for a lawman of his calibre to bother pursuing these robbers.

There was a knock at the door.

'Come in,' Bain shouted.

The door opened, and Madeleine Brightman, the telegraph operator's wife, stood there nervously, no doubt awed in Bain's presence.

'Come in, I said,' Bain barked. 'Are you deaf as well as ugly, woman?'

Mrs Brightman entered sheepishly. She was holding one of the telegraph forms on which the operator wrote down the messages. She stood there, not saying a word.

Bain gave her a hard, steely stare. 'You can leave now, you stupid woman. Get out of my sight.'

She turned, and began to leave.

'And shut the door on the way out!'

When the door was closed, Bain turned his attention to the message.

It read:

APPLETON INSURANCE COMPANY TO NATHAN BAIN.

RECEIVED YOUR INSTRUCTIONS RE CANCELLATION OF BANK INSURANCE. STOP. POLICY NOW TERMINATED. STOP. SORRY TO LOSE YOUR BUSINESS. STOP.

Bain thought, *What the hell? No. This can't be.* This was

the key part of the plan. There was no point in stealing his own money if he wasn't going to be compensated for the theft by the insurance company.

How could this have happened? He was certain that Jesse James and his men could be trusted. They had to have been overawed by the sheer magnificence of Nathan Bain. Abernathy must have tricked them somehow, stolen the money away from them and arranged to get the insurance policy cancelled.

Where were the deputies? *If only Cal were here*, Bain thought. Then he remembered – he had fired Cal.

Without the deputies, he would have to investigate this himself. Since he knew he was the greatest lawman in the territory, it wouldn't be too hard for him.

He went out, loped along the boardwalk to the telegraph office and barged through the door. He strode up to Abe Brightman, and stood menacingly over him.

'What's the meaning of this, Abe?' he said, thrusting the telegraph message towards Abe.

Abe picked it up and looked at it. 'Why, that's the reply to the wire you sent to the insurance company, cancelling your policy.'

'That *I* sent. . . ?' Bain shouted and spluttered. 'I never did any such thing. You're a liar and a cheat, and if you don't explain yourself this instant I'm going to take you to the jail house and lock you up.'

Abe said, 'But Mr Bain. I was only carrying out your instructions. Young Geoffrey came in a coupla days ago. He gave me the message, said it was from you. So I sent it.'

Bain frowned. *Geoffrey? Who's that?* Then he remembered the bellboy in the hotel who'd disappeared the same time that Abernathy had done a bunk.

Bain roared with indignation. 'Yah idiot, Brightman! That boy quit before I could fire him. I was going to arrest him for criminal activity but he escaped. Did you not think to check with me first?'

'You never told me that he'd gone,' Abe said. 'I thought he was still at the hotel. He was in his uniform. I had no reason not to send the wire.'

A sudden whooshing went over Bain's head. He felt his hat flying off his head. He ducked down, not because he was afraid, no, but to make himself a smaller target.

'Are you all right, Mr Bain?'

Bain looked up. It was Abe, hovering over him.

'Why wouldn't I be all right? And what business is it of yours?'

'Somebody fired an arrow into this office. That is my business.'

Bain looked up, and saw the arrow in the wall. He stayed crouched down, and crawled nearer to the arrow. It was just like the one in his own office, except that this one had his hat skewered on it, as well as a piece of paper. He tore the paper from the arrow and stuffed it quickly into his pants pocket.

'And Abe? Send a wire to the insurance company again, advising them that the cancellation of the insurance policy should be *rekindled*.'

Although he wasn't sure what Bain meant by 'rekindled', Abe knew he didn't dare ask, so he just nodded in agreement. 'Will do, Mr Bain. Shall I add the cost to the sheriff's office account?'

Bain glared at him. 'Just do it, or I'll put yuh under arrest.'

Abe sat down at the telegraph key.

Bain had no time to wait to make sure that Abe sent the message, and hurriedly ran back to his office. His hand shook as he inserted the key into the lock. *This damned dyspepsia*, he thought, *must be putting me out of sorts.*

He managed to get the door opened, dashed through, and then locked it again from the inside. He looked at the note, but it was blurred. He put on the eyeglasses that he didn't need and saw that it was another note from that odious Abernathy. What kind of name was Abernathy, anyway? A phony baloney alias for sure. The guy's name must really be Flint Andrews, and he was some kind of criminal mastermind.

The note read: 'We're on to you, Swiggard. Come alone. Be at the disused swing station by five o'clock if you want to see your money again.'

Bain howled. He felt his eyes watering, something must have been wrong with the steak he'd had at lunch.

Bain looked at the clock on the wall. Half past three. If he waited for Savage and the other deputies to return, he wouldn't make it to the swing station on time. He realized that he would have to go by himself to the meet with this Abernathy, or Andrews, or whatever his name was. Perhaps something could be salvaged from this after all. Every man had his price, and it was just a matter of offering the writer a deal. Either that, or blow his brains out.

Bain was convinced that everything was going to be all right.

Bain added a rifle boot to his saddle pack before setting off to meet with the insane criminal who had dared to thwart him.

After riding for about an hour, he reached the low

ridge that marked the boundary of his jurisdiction in the county. He rode to the top, knowing that this would bring him within sight of Cripple Creek station. Wells Fargo had used this place for many years, but a bigger staging post had been built some five miles north, with more facilities, allowing overnight stays for passengers. Bain had campaigned for Misery to be used for such purposes, but for some reason Wells Fargo preferred to build out in the middle of nowhere. Who could figure it? What was wrong with Misery?

He saw four horses hitched to a still-upright rail of the ruined corral, but didn't see any signs of any men there.

He rode down and about fifteen minutes later he approached the station. No point in stealth. He would have to rely on his superior abilities to get the better of these criminals. He felt a shiver run through him and thought that the effects of that steak he'd eaten hadn't quite worn off yet.

Gunn watched from the broken window of the station as Swiggard approached. He saw that he wasn't wearing his usual white hat. He wore a black Stetson, which looked too small for his head.

As Swiggard approached the ruined building, Gunn stepped out through the doorway, and took aim with a Winchester.

'You can stop there, Swiggard,' Gunn shouted out as the big man arrived at the broken posts and rails of the corral. Swiggard gave Gunn a contemptuous stare, but stopped.

'Who's Swiggard? And who might you be?' Swiggard asked. 'I don't think that I've ever seen yuh before.'

'You have, though. You have that.'

'I think I would have remembered. That collar yuh're wearing? Are yuh some kind of priest?'

'Don't insult me. I'm a minister of the Church of Scotland.'

'Scotland? That's part of England, isn't it?'

'No. Make another remark like that and I'll blow your head off.'

'What did I say?' Swiggard said.

Abernathy stepped out of the doorway. He was holding a Colt .45, rather awkwardly.

'Just step off the horse, Swiggard,' Abernathy said. 'No sudden movements, and keep your hands where we can see them at all times.'

Swiggard jumped down from his mount, surprisingly agile for such a big man. Abernathy stepped forward swiftly and removed Swiggard's revolver from its holster before the big man had a chance to react.

'Yuh keep calling me Swiggard,' he said. 'I don't get it. Who is this man Swiggard?'

'You are,' Gunn said.

'I think yuh've mistaken me for someone else.'

'Give it up, Mark.' Cal Cannon stepped through the doorway. 'Everybody here knows who you really are.'

Swiggard frowned. 'Cal? You're dead.'

'Apparently not,' Cal said.

Swiggard glared at his former deputy. 'Yuh're a filthy traitor. I knew I should never have trusted a nig—'

Cal stepped towards Swiggard, and punched him, hard in the face, breaking his nose. Swiggard squealed and put his hand to his nose. Blood trickled down his arm.

'You stinking coward!' Swiggard shouted.

'I've been wanting to do that for a long time,' Cal said.

'Where's mah money?' Swiggard asked.

Jesse James stepped from the doorway and said, 'What do you mean, *your* money? We stole it, fair and square.'

'That wasn't our deal. Yuh can have half a per cent, like we agreed.'

'I don't think so,' Jesse said. 'You were planning to have your deputies come with you to collect the money, then when we handed it over they would kill us. You're getting precisely none of the money. Or the insurance.'

'I've sent a wire to the insurance company, telling them that the previous message cancelling the policy was a fake.'

'Do you know that this wire was sent?' Abernathy asked.

A look of puzzlement flashed in Swiggard's eyes. 'What d'yuh mean?'

Brendan stepped forward, and said, 'I went to the telegraph office before you did, and bribed Abe not to send any message from you. Cost fifty dollars, but it was worth it.'

Swiggard glared at Brendan.

'Yuh're just a stupid kid. Where would yah get fifty dollars?'

'From the proceeds of the robbery.'

'Once I get back to town, I'll force Abe to send the message.'

Gunn said, 'No, you won't. To get back to town, you'll have to kill all of us.'

'I'm the greatest shootist in the territory. Yuh wouldn't stand a chance.'

Frank stepped towards the sheriff, and offered his gun back to him. Swiggard looked at it, then at Frank, as if he couldn't believe how stupid these outlaws were. He took the gun, and cocked the hammer.

'Why are yuh doing this?' he asked.

'Do you recognize me?' Gunn asked.

'No. Yuh talk kinda funny. Are yuh French?'

Gunn cast a sidelong glance at Abernathy, who rolled his eyes.

'No, I'm not French. I'm Scottish, and I speak the guid Scots tongue.'

'I don't know yuh.'

'Let me refresh your memory. You bushwhacked me, stole my horse and left me for dead.'

'Not me.'

'I'd know your face anywhere,' the Scotsman said.

Brendan said, 'You killed my family. Over a decade ago.'

Swiggard looked blank.

Brendan continued: 'A homestead in the Dakota territory. Not far from the Lakota reservation.'

'Not me. I'm a war hero, and the most upright and fearless lawman in the whole of the west.'

Cal sniggered.

Joseph said, 'And three years before that, you massacred a Lakota encampment, almost in the same spot where you bushwhacked Mr Gunn.'

Swiggard was shaking with rage. 'How dare yuh! I'm a holder of the Congressional Medal of Honour.'

'If you are,' Abernathy said, 'it's because you stole one. I researched the real Nathan Bain, and he *was* a war hero, but that's not a medal that he won. He was nominated for it, but the War Department rejected the recommendation.'

'Liar. Who do yuh think you are, yuh lily-livered pansy

scribbler? I could lick yuh any day of the week.'

Swiggard aimed his gun at the writer. Abernathy snorted, and turned his back on him.

'Give it up, Mark,' Cal said. 'I've told them all about you. They know exactly who you are.'

'What did I ever do to you, yuh traitorous little snot?'

'You get a sadist like Savage and morons like Billson and Watney to kill people, and you think it's funny.'

'I'm not a crook,' Swiggard said.

'Yes, you are,' Jesse said. 'It's people like you who give crooks like me a bad name.'

'Who do yuh think yuh're talking to, yuh pipsqueak? I'm not a crook, but if I were, I'd be a lot better at it than you are, you and your mangy brother.'

Frank said, 'Pity Cal has already busted your nose. My mangy fist could easily break it again.'

Joseph said, 'You *are* a crook, and a murderer. I saw you and your gang murder everybody at a Lakota encampment, all except me.'

'Liar!' Swiggard shouted, almost screaming. His face was turning purple with rage. 'Yuh're nothing but a punk kid, and a redskin. Nobody could ever trust the word of an Indian.'

'*We* all do,' Gunn said. 'Let's finish this now. You're not getting the money back, but we're going to give you one chance to live.'

'What do yuh mean, "live"? You can't kill me. I'm the sheriff of Misery. Hundreds of gunslicks and outlaws have tried, but they're all in jail or under the ground. I beat them all.'

Cal said, 'The only crooks in Misery were you, me and the other deputies. Only drunks and fine defaulters ever spent any time in jail. Why don't you listen to the deal that Mr Gunn is offering you?'

Swiggard shrugged. 'I might as well listen to your idiocy before I kill the lot of yuh.'

Gunn said, 'We're going to fight a duel, Swiggard. Just you and me. But it's not going to be the quick-draw style you westerners seem so fond of. It's going to be the way it used to be done in the British Isles before it was outlawed by Act of Parliament.'

'What do yuh mean?'

'We stand back to back. On the count of three, we take five paces away from each other. Mr Abernathy will do the count, then he will count our paces. When he counts to five, we turn, and shoot at each other.'

'And if I don't agree?'

Abernathy said, 'Then we strip you naked, tie you to a tree, and leave you. I hear there are coyotes in these parts. . . .'

Swiggard shivered, then threw up.

After he'd recovered himself, he said, 'Must've been something I ate. I agree to the duel.'

'Very well then,' Gunn said, and nodded to his companions.

Brendan and Joseph held Swiggard and led him into position, because they knew that the coward couldn't be trusted to follow the instructions. Gunn stepped up to them to take his position.

'Lemme go, yuh punks,' Swiggard said.

'No,' Brendan said. 'Not until Mr Abernathy has counted to five.'

Jesse handed Gunn a revolver, which he holstered. Abernathy handed Joseph an identical gun, and Joseph slipped that into Swiggard's holster.

'What's with the guns?' Swiggard asked.

Abernathy said, 'Since this is a duel, there's only one round in the chamber. It will move into firing position when you cock the hammer. We're not cheats, we're giving you a chance, fair and square.'

'What happens if I kill this fool?'

'We'll let you go,' Abernathy said. 'But I've written a true account of Mark Swiggard and Nathan Bain, and I've had it printed up, and it's being delivered to everybody in Misery. Whatever happens, you're finished in this territory.'

'Let's get on with it,' Gunn said.

Abernathy said, 'On three, step forward five paces. One. Two. Three.'

Gunn started moving. Swiggard also stepped forward, with Brendan and Joseph keeping tight hold of him. Abernathy counted the paces, and as he reached 'five', the two boys let Swiggard go and stepped away from him.

Swiggard drew his gun as he turned. He felt a slight dizziness from the rapid motion, and hesitated until Gunn came into focus. He saw that the clergyman had not drawn his gun, and was standing with his hands clasped behind his head.

Was this man a fool? Was this some kind of trick?

'What the hell are yuh doing, preacher man?' Swiggard asked.

'I'm trusting in God.'

'Then you are a fool. God won't stop me from putting a bullet in your brain.'

'Go ahead then.'

Swiggard still tried to work out the catch. Gunn and the

others made no move. Swiggard looked around, but couldn't figure out what kind of trick they were trying to pull.

Then he cocked the hammer, and pulled the trigger.

And missed. The bullet whizzed about five feet wide of Gunn, and embedded itself into the wall of the station.

'Same old Mark,' Cal said. 'Never could shoot worth a damn.'

Swiggard glared at Cal. 'I'm going to kill you, you traitorous scum.'

He reached down and took out a concealed gun from his boot, then he pointed it at Cal and fired twice. The second slug caught Cal in the forearm, and he screamed with the pain of the impact and fell to the ground.

Gunn took his hands down from his head and in an instant his gun was out of its holster, cocked, and fired, and the bullet went plumb into the middle of Swiggard's forehead.

'May God forgive you your sins, Swiggard,' Gunn said. 'I certainly don't.'

And that was the last thing that Swiggard heard, before he fell backwards into the dust and died.

CHAPTER SIXTEEN

The party came back to town, minus Cal and Joseph, who had gone to the Lazy H to seek medical attention for Cal's wound.

The town was eerily quiet as they rode in. They stopped at the undertaker, to drop off the corpse. Dan Gentry, the coffin maker, came to see what business had been brought his way. When he saw who the corpse was, he rubbed his hands.

'So that bastard Bain is dead at last. I'd like to shake the hand of the man who did that.'

Gunn dismounted and said, 'That would be me.'

Gentry looked at Gunn, and saw his clerical collar. 'Well, padre, I suppose there's some justice in Bain being killed by a man of God.'

Gunn shook Gentry's hand, but then said, 'Nathan Bain died long ago, killed by Mr Savage on this monster's orders. This creature is named Mark Swiggard.'

Gentry said, 'I never figured how this critter could have been a war hero. Always struck me as a swaggering clown. Never dared to go against him, though. Paid up all the taxes because I knew what his deputies would do if I didn't.'

'Well, you won't need to worry about him again.'

'What about the deputies?'

Gunn said, 'We hope to get rid of them, too.'

'Where are they?' the undertaker asked.

'They're leading a posse chasing after the bank robbers,' Abernathy said.

Gentry shrugged. 'I wouldn't like to be in the robbers' shoes if those deputies catch up with them.'

'Well, they haven't caught up with us yet,' Frank said.

Gentry looked puzzled.

'We're the bank robbers,' Jesse said. 'We weren't stealing the money from the town, we were stealing it from the sheriff. We've brought it all back. Well, nearly all.'

'Bring Swagger – or whatever his name is – inside, and I'll measure him up for a coffin.'

The James brothers dragged the corpse into the shop, where Gentry instructed them to place it onto a table.

'I'd do this one for free,' he said, 'but a corpse that size is going to need a bigger coffin than usual. He's still getting the cheapest wood I can find.'

Gunn said, 'A pleasure doing business with you.'

'Good man, padre. And what's your name?'

'Gunn. Guthrie Gunn.'

'Well, Mr Gunn, that sure is a different way of drumming up business for yourself. You kill them, then you can say the prayers when we're putting them in the grave.'

'Not this one. My only prayer for this one is that he goes to the hell I don't believe in.'

Gentry looked askance. 'Rum kind of preacher, if you ask me.'

Gunn plucked the sheriff's star from Swiggard's vest, and attached it to his own waistcoat.

'Looks like I've appointed myself the sheriff of Misery. At least for today.'

'You've got my vote,' Gentry said.

Gunn and the others bid their farewells to Gentry. Leaving the undertaker, they split up. Abernathy took the loot away, and Frank and Geoffrey went with him to the bank.

Gunn set off with Jesse and Brendan, stepping across the street to the sheriff's office. It didn't open, but rather than going back to the undertaker to look for the key on Swiggard's corpse, Jesse shot the lock off.

Once inside, Gunn sat down in the sheriff's chair. Jesse took the other chair, while Brendan kept a lookout from the doorway.

Gunn rummaged in the desk, and plucked two tin stars from a drawer, pushed one over the desk towards Jesse, and threw the other to Brendan.

Jesse looked at it warily, never having had one offered to him before.

Gunn said, 'By the powers invested in me by . . . um . . . me, I'm appointing you both as my deputies.'

'I don't rightly know, Guthrie. Nobody's ever offered me a position as a deputy before.'

'Go on, Joshua. It's only for today. It'll do you good to be on the right side of the law for once.'

Jesse looked at the star, then picked it up and pinned it onto his vest. Then he chuckled. 'Jesse James, deputy sheriff. Who'da thought it?'

Brendan pinned his star on, and said, 'Jesse, you look the part more than that guy Savage does.'

Jesse raised his eyebrows. 'What do we do now, Guthrie?'

'We wait. We wait for the posse to come back.

'And what then?'

'Then we throw Savage and Billson and Watney into jail.'

'And if they resist?'

The preacher said, 'I'm sure we'll think of something,' his hand rubbing the butt of his gun.

Abernathy led the way into the bank. Striding to the counter, he placed the sack on top of it. The teller looked at him quizzically.

'What can I do for you, sir?' the teller said.

'I'd like to make a deposit.'

'Certainly, sir. Do you have an account with us.'

'No.'

'Do you wish to open an account?'

'No.'

'I don't see how we can accept a deposit without an account.'

'You'll want to accept this.'

The other teller was looking on with puzzlement and some nervousness. He still had a bruise on his jaw from the previous day.

'How much do you wish to deposit, sir?'

'Approximately fifty thousand dollars.'

The teller picked up a pen to write the amount on a deposit slip. Then dropped it, giving Abernathy a hard stare.

'More or less. It's the loot from yesterday's robbery. There might be a few hundred dollars missing, but other than that it's all there in this sack.'

'Does Mr Bain know about this?' the teller said.

'Not exactly. Nathan Bain died some years ago, killed by Randall Savage.'

'I don't understand.'

Abernathy said, 'The man you knew as Nathan Bain was an impostor named Mark Swiggard. He knew that the bank was going to be robbed . . . he was in on the plan.'

'Sheriff Bain . . . is dead?'

'Mark Swiggard. But definitely dead. His body is with the undertaker right now.'

'That's the best news I've heard in years.'

'What's your name, lad?' Abernathy asked.

'Brett Westwood.'

'Good name. I think I'll steal it for one of my novels.'

'Sir?'

'Never mind.'

'Would you like a receipt for this money?'

'Since it's not mine, it wouldn't be right for me to get a receipt. The money belongs to the people of Misery. But I'll stay here while you count it. And so will the gentlemen with me.'

'Very well, sir.'

So the tellers counted it. The total came to $49,515.

Frank whispered to Abernathy, 'Damn near fifty thousand, and we're giving it back. Doesn't seem right, somehow.'

The new temporary sheriff and his two deputies waited patiently in the sheriff's office.

As they waited, Gunn and Jesse swapped stories, with Gunn speaking of his life in Scotland, and Jesse telling of

149

his experiences in the war and his career as an outlaw.

Gunn tutted at the tales of marauding with Quantrill's Raiders, and the subsequent career as a criminal, but Jesse knew that the Scotsman was impressed.

After more than an hour, the thundering noise of hoof beats approached. Brendan nodded from his lookout position, and as the riders approached he moved further back into the room, so that he wouldn't be seen by the approaching deputies.

Brendan said, 'Looks like the deputies have sent the volunteers from the posse away. It's just the three of them coming.'

'Ready, Joshua?' Gunn asked.

Jesse said, 'I'm ready,' and he stood up and walked to the other side of the sheriff's desk, then turned to face the doorway. Brendan nocked an arrow, and aimed it at the door.

Moments later, the door was flung open and Randall Savage barged in. Without really looking, he began to speak.

'Boss, I did like yuh tole me. Led the posse in the wrong direction, long enough to convince 'em that we were after the robbers. Then I tole 'em that we'd lost the trail, and. . . .'

His eyes came into focus, and he saw that the sheriff wasn't Swiggard.

'Who the hell are you?'

'There's a new sheriff in town, laddie, and it's me.'

'Where's Bain?'

'In the undertakers.'

'Whut's he doin' there?' Savage growled. Then realized, and said, 'Oh! Wus it a heart attack?'

'In a way. His heart stopped, all right, after I put a bullet in his brain.'

'And who made you the sheriff?'

'God appointed me,' Gunn said.

Savage wrinkled his nose in puzzlement, then looked around and took in the presence of Jesse James and Brendan.

'And who are these guys?'

'They are my deputies.'

Savage scoffed. 'This town already has deputies. With Bain dead. . . .'

'Swiggard,' Gunn said.

Savage snarled at the Scotsman. 'With Bain dead, that makes me the acting sheriff.'

'No,' Gunn said. 'We're arresting you for murder.'

Savage laughed. 'Murder? Who did I murder?'

Brendan said, 'The Brennan family.'

'Who?'

'My ma and pa and my sister.'

'His mother was also my sister,' Gunn added.

'Never killed nobody that didn't need killing.'

'And you also killed several Lakota tribesmen, massacred them in their tepees.'

'Injuns, huh?' Savage scoffed. 'Never met one yet wasn't better off dead.'

Brendan restrained himself from loosing an arrow at the man.

Gunn said, 'Put down your gun, and we'll put you in a cell.'

Savage moved his hands slowly towards the buckle of his gun-belt. Then in a rapid motion his gun was in his hand, and he got off two shots.

The slugs whizzed past the Scotsman's ear, and thwacked into the wall at the back of the office.

Brendan let loose an arrow, which caught Savage in the throat. Blood spurted from his mouth, and he fell to the floor.

Billson and Watney arrived at the open doorway and were baffled to see Savage on the floor with an arrow in his throat. They drew their guns and fired a couple of shots each. Which missed.

'Put down your weapons and surrender,' Gunn said.

The only reply was a slug from the gun of Billson, which clipped the preacher's left earlobe. Gunn blasted Billson three times, full in the chest. Billson fell on top of Savage, snapping Brendan's arrow as he went down.

Watney dropped his gun, raised his hands in the air. 'I surrender. Don't kill me.'

'First sensible thing any of you has said,' Jesse said.

'Would you care to put this reprobate in a cell, Joshua?' Gunn said.

Jesse said, 'Reprobate, huh? You do talk fancy for a sheriff. It'd be my pleasure.'

Jesse led Watney to the cells, shoved him into one, then locked the door. As Jesse came back to give Gunn the key, Abernathy came in.

'My, you *have* been busy,' he said. 'Sorry I missed it. I'll want a full description of what happened here so that I can use it.'

'Buy me a drink, preferably a twenty-year-old malt whisky, and I'll tell you the whole story.'

'You've been shot,' Abernathy said.

Gunn put his hand up to his ear, and then looked at the bloodstain on his finger. He shrugged. 'Just a scratch. It doesn't hurt.'

'Well, there's blood dripping onto your collar.'

'That'll wash off.' He wiped the blood on his finger on his waistcoat. Then took off the star pinned to it.

'I hereby resign as sheriff,' he said. Then he offered the star to Jesse. 'Here, Joshua, would you like to be sheriff for a while.'

Jesse said, 'This law enforcement is some career, beats robbing banks. I've only been a deputy for about an hour, and now I'm being offered the post of sheriff.'

'Do you accept?'

'Naw. Deputy's one thing, but how would it look if word ever got around that Jesse James had been a sheriff. I'd become a laughing stock.'

'Well, I suppose there's a vacancy in town now.'

'Let the townspeople sort it out.'

'What about you, Brendan? Would you like to be sheriff?'

'No, thanks. If you don't need me, I'm going to go back to the Lazy H, to see how Joseph is. And. . . .'

Gunn noted the boy's hesitation. 'And?'

Brendan said, 'And I'm going to ask Emmy to marry me.'

EPILOGUE

'Dearly beloved . . .'

The congregation waited, hushed.

'Who am I kidding?' Gunn said. 'I know there's an order of service that I'm meant to follow, but it really only applies under the laws of Scotland. I don't know much about laws in Montana Territory, but because I'm an ordained clergyman my conducting the ceremony makes it legal. Whatever the form of words.

'I'm certainly not going to use the Book of Common Prayer, the Anglicans get far too much of their own way as it is. But all it needs for the ceremony to be legal is for me to ask if there's any legal obstacle preventing these two people from being married to each other, for them to consent to be husband and wife, and according to the laws of Scotland I have to use the words "husband" and "wife". I'm certainly not going to avoid that just because there's nae Scottish jurisdiction here.

'I also have to ask whether anybody here knows of any just cause or impediment preventing this man and this woman from joining together in wedlock.'

Gunn paused, then continued. 'Good. I'm not currently wearing a firearm because I'm doing ministry for the Lord, but if any man had spoken up there I'd have gone to get my gun and then shot him.'

Gunn paused again and waited until the congregation started laughing.

Gunn smiled. 'That's that settled, then. Now we come to the bit where the Anglicans do the plighting of troth. I'm not an Anglican, the groom's not an Anglican. He's a Papist, and I'm not sure if that's worse. Is the bride an Anglican?'

Emmeline said, 'No, sir. I'm a Methodist.'

Gunn grinned. 'That's definitely worse than an Anglican. We're all Christians here, except the best man, and he shows more Christian charity than I do. Where was I? We'll not do plighting each other's troth, it's not a legal requirement. Shall we do consenting to marry?'

Brendan and Emmeline nodded.

Gunn went on: 'OK, Brendan. Repeat after me. I, Brendan Michael Brennan . . .'

'I, Brendan Michael Brennan . . .

'. . . do avow that I take you . . .'

'. . . do avow that I take you . . .'

'. . . Emmeline Catherine Hardin . . .'

'. . . Emmeline Catherine Hardin . . .'

'. . . to be my lawful wedded wife.'

'. . . to be my lawful wedded wife.'

'Well done, Brendan. Now, Emmeline, you can repeat after me. I, Emmeline Catherine Hardin . . .'

'I, Emmeline Catherine Hardin . . .'

'. . . do avow that I take you . . .'

'. . . do avow that I take you . . .'

'. . . Brendan Michael Brennan . . .'

'. . . Brendan Michael Brennan . . .'

'. . . to be my lawful wedded husband.'

'. . . to be my lawful wedded husband.'

'That's great, Emmy,' Gunn said. 'We've been using those words "husband" and "wife" a lot, so that's definitely legal. What's next? Oh, the ring. Now you don't have to have a ring, or you can have one for the bride, or you can have one each. Doesn't make the ceremony any less legal, whichever you choose. But I see Joseph has taken his hand out of his pocket, and now he's holding a ring between his thumb and index finger. OK laddie, give the ring to Brendan.'

Joseph handed it over. Brendan took Emmy's left hand.

'OK, Brendan. Put the ring on her finger. We'll not do that stuff about worshipping her body, that's all Church of England guff. I know you love her and she loves you . . .'

Brendan slipped the ring onto Emmy's finger.

'One last bit and we're done.

'Do you, Brendan, take this woman to be your lawful wedded wife?'

'I do.'

'Do you, Emmeline, take this man to be your lawful wedded husband?'

'I do.' Emmy beamed radiantly.

The dour Scotsman in Gunn found it sickening that anybody could seem so happy. As her new uncle by marriage, he was just as happy as she was, but wouldn't let it show on his face.

'Then by the powers invested in me by God, our saviour Jesus Christ, and the Church of Scotland, and in accordance with the laws of the Territory of Montana, et cetera et cetera, I pronounce you husband and wife.'

Nobody spoke, nobody moved.

'Well then, Brendan. What are you waiting for? Kiss the new Mrs Brennan right now, or I'll exercise my prerogative as your uncle and kiss her first.'

Brendan kissed Emmy, then kissed her again. Then he shook his uncle's hand.

'The only thing remaining is for Mr and Mrs Brennan to sign the legal papers, which will be witnessed by me as the presiding clergyman, and by two other witnesses. The papers are waiting for us in the library. The newly married couple can walk down the aisle together, and we'll sign the papers, then this room can be cleared of all the chairs so that we can use it for one hell of a party.'

Joseph went to the piano, started playing Mendelssohn's Wedding March, as was the new fashion, and Brendan and Emmy walked up the aisle, to loud cheering from the assembled congregation.

There's not much more left to tell.

The party at the Hardin ranch to celebrate the wedding of Brendan Brennan and Emmeline Hardin was a grand affair, and they do say, nearly three decades on, that it was the finest shindig ever seen in Cornwall County. I should know – I was there. It was hard to believe that a humble dime novelist, who could now just about ride a horse, and still can't shoot (never been able to hit what I aim at, despite twenty-five years of practising), could have been part of the gang who brought down Swiggard.

The party was the last time that Gunn's Avengers were all together. The James brothers left the next day, and I promised them that I would write the true story of their time in Misery. I did, but the publishers changed it. The book that I titled The Legend of Misery by Frederick Abernathy, became *Mayhem in Montana*, credited to Flint Anderson, and Jesse and Frank were depicted as villains, duped into fighting the heroic sheriff Nathaniel Bradley by the evil Indian Roaring Buffalo. There was a drunken Scotsman, George Gourlay, who was there as comic relief. I was too ashamed to send a copy to Jesse and Frank, it was such a travesty. I would make a real effort to learn to shoot if I thought I could get away with killing the creatures who rewrote my story.

I never got to write the true story of the James gang. I was set to travel west to interview Jesse and Frank when I learned that Jesse had been killed by a traitor in the gang. I did meet Frank some years later, but he didn't have the heart to be interviewed about his life, and would only talk about our adventures in Montana.

Brendan settled down at the Hardin ranch, adopted Clemmy and he and Emmy raised another four children. When Chase Hardin retired from ranching to go into local politics, Brendan took over the ownership of the ranch, and the last I heard it's still flourishing, and Guthrie Brennan is learning the trade to take over from his father when the time comes.

Joseph Brennan became Kicking Buffalo again, and returned to the tribal reservation in Dakota. He became an important chief.

Guthrie Gunn stayed in the west, travelling the land and preaching to the converted and unconverted alike. After having been bushwhacked by Swiggard and his gang, he was reluctant to travel alone. Having lost his two faithful companions, he took up with the unlikeliest of Sancho

Panzas, Caleb Cannon. The man who had been one of his bushwhackers became his right-hand man, and was his travelling companion for some years. And less likely than that, Geoffrey had joined them, too. I heard Gunn has settled down now, weary from years on the road. But I can hardly believe it, in fact I won't believe it until he writes to me in person confirming it.

As for me, well I'd like to tell you that I became a successful novelist, lauded by a grateful reading public, but as I mentioned at the beginning, you probably never heard of me. But in Cornwall County in Montana, they remember me. I've been back a few times since those days, when the vagaries of my income permitted, and Misery is a flourishing town now that it's free of the corruption of Swiggard and his gang. The townsfolk have renamed it Mercy, the correct translation of the original Latin name its Jesuit founder gave it. The people of Mercy are mostly decent men and women, and such is their regard for me that they told me that they would vote for me if I stood for the position of mayor of Mercy. I told them I was a registered Democrat, and that still didn't bother them. It was a tempting offer, but I felt I had to decline. I'm a scribbler by trade, and it's all that I know. I thought that politics should be left to the politicians.

But I got a letter from Emmy Brennan recently, writing on behalf of her father, who wants to step down as mayor of Mercy after three terms, but the town assembly won't let him retire unless I agree to take his place. Emmy and her father know my previously stated opinions on the matter, but they're begging me to reconsider. Now that I've got some more maturity, and (I like to think) a bit of wisdom, and I'm married now with three almost-grown children of my own, I'm a different man now from the one who was once the least of Gunn's Avengers. I spoke to my wife and the children about it, and they were agreed about what I should do, so I've written back to Emmy telling her that we're coming, and coming to stay.

Who knows? Perhaps finally after all these years somebody will be able to teach me how to shoot.